Marcus Youssef, Mary Swan & John Lavery

COMING ATTRACTIONS
99

This book was published with the assistance of the Canada Council and others. We acknowledge the support of the Canada Council for the Arts and the Government of Canada through the Book Publishing Industry Development Program for our publishing activities. Canadä

Acknowledgements: "By the Sea, By the Sea" by Mary Swan first appeared in *The Ontario Review* and "On the Border" by Mary Swan was originally published in *Carousel Magazine*. "You, Judith Kamada" by John Lavery was first published in *The Antigonish Review*, "The Breeze Being Needed" by John Lavery originally appeared in *Prism International*, and "Naming Darkness" by John Lavery was first published in *The Fiddlehead*.

ISBN 0 7780 1122 4 (hardcover)
ISBN 0 7780 1123 2 (softcover)

Cover art by Edgar Degas
Book design by Michael Macklem

Printed in Canada

PUBLISHED IN CANADA BY OBERON PRESS

Contents

THESE THREE NEW writers—Marcus Youssef, Mary Swan and John Lavery—are all, in some ways, talking about how we make ourselves, how we create our identities.

Marcus Youssef, who has already begun to make a name for himself as a playwright, approaches the question with a dramatist's eye and a real comic gift. But there is a sting beneath the humour in his three stories, linked by a tense, troubled and all-too-self-aware central character. Racial, sexual and family politics twist together into engaging and disturbing knots, as the protagonist tries to locate himself as his father's son, his mother's son, a man, a husband, a father. "My name is written in Toller's aggressively round print across the top," the narrator Jason tells us in "More Like a Person (In My Country)." "It's mis-spelled, as usual. Jason Ab*u*-Mouss*e*, it says, which I translate roughly to mean Jason, father of fluffy chocolate dessert. Ab*a* Mouss*a*, my real name, means son of Moussa, though I am not son of Moussa, I am son of Paul. Moussa was my grandfather, a doctor who killed himself after losing everything betting on Egyptian cotton futures in the fifties."

Mary Swan's stories are quieter, more reflective. She takes small, strange incidents—from a young woman who died of "overbathing" to the simple act of changing a lightbulb—and develops them into meditations of a sort; thoughts about how our past shapes our future, as individuals and as a community. "Someone should know about Mary McIntyre," she writes, "and yet it's so hard to keep her in focus. Her outline blurs, as it does in those photographs, as she herself faded out. The sound of her voice no more than a murmur against the tinkling of silver spoons on saucers, the competing bands from the park, the pier, from the great hall of the Kursaal." Swan evokes those murmurs, and brings us to hear them.

John Lavery writes with the most striking diversity of voices—from Ossama, a young boy "of Egyptian distraction" moving between Canada and the United States, to Daphne MacMillan, Associate of the Royal Conservatory of Music, whose life and pain we follow through her relationship with her blind student Janice. Lavery's stories are dark and sometimes bizarre, but they move with a tremendous energy, often through unexpected events. He writes, finally, about powerful attachments between people—maybe not always what we can call love, but difficult obsessions, devotions and loyalties, and the ways that they shape us. "I have my name. Not that it matters because you won't like my name. And anyway my darkness will really be a lightness won't it. ...But I might as well tell you its name will be very good butter. Do you like it? ...Very good butter. No, well I told you you wouldn't."

MAGGIE HELWIG

Contributions for *Coming Attractions* 2000, published or unpublished, should be sent directly to Oberon Press at 400–350 Sparks Street, Ottawa, Ontario KIR 7S8 before 31 December 1999. All manuscripts should be accompanied by a stamped, self-addressed envelope.

MARCUS YOUSSEF

Icebreaking

J wants to go down, that's the truth of it.

Gerry was doing a dance, raising his right fist in the air. The song was a tinny emanation from a cream-coloured am-fm clock-radio and the lads at the table ignored him.

"I can't get no...mmm, mmm, mm, mmm!"

"You guys, man," J said from his stoner's slump on the legless vinyl chair in the corner. "Oh, Jesus, you know what?" he added suddenly, sitting upright for the first time in an hour or more (he couldn't exactly remember).

"Sa-aa-tiz-fack-sh-"

The guys looked up at him over their cards.

"The students."

Lads returned to their game, except Gerry who, fist suspended in the air, left the final syllable of the chorus unconsummated.

"I just realized, they're down there by themselves."

"What about Katie?" Gerry asked

"She's staying at Claire's."

Gerry furrowed his brow in an overdone, muppety gesture of concern. "Yeah," he said, nodding severely six or seven times. "That's true."

"I should go down there," said J.

"You think so?" Gerry asked.

It took J a moment to make sense of the ringing noise from next to the clock radio. A phone. An old one. With a bell.

Gerry reached across the table to grab it.

"Film school," he said brightly. He had an extension put into his house, so he could sleep late, play bridge on Monday nights and perpetually foster the illusion that he's at work. Which he is. 24-7. Gramby Island's token workaholic, he even convinced what's left of the National Film Board to kick in 25 grand a summer. To work with kids.

"Uh, huh? Oh, yeah. Oh, Jesus, really. Okay. No, thanks, Sue, I appreciate it. Kids, eh. No, it's okay, one of my teachers is about to go down anyway, he'll check it out. Cheers!"

Hoisting his can of Lucky Lager, Gerry smiled. It was the woman who runs the island internet server. "One of the kids has been using our computer to log on to some porn sites. She thought we ought to know."

"Oh, fuck me," said J squeezing down the last urinary gulp of a Heineken, his purchase of which was the subject of much ribaldric amusement, before.

The guys laughed.

The two stories, the one in unfolding in front of him and the one in his head, were starting to mix, airily.

"Maybe you should go down there," said Gerry, thoughtfully, the implications maybe, just maybe, beginning to penetrate his overarching love of the Stones. The school ran for three summers before one of the instructors convinced him that it might be prudent to purchase some insurance.

"Yeah. If something happened and there was no-one down there to deal with it, we'd be in big trouble," J said.

"Yeah. Absolutely. Thanks."

"Is there a flashlight?"

Gerry opened his mouth like a flytrap, then closed it again.

"Flashlight. Right."

He shuffled around the crusty kitchen until he spied something on top of the fridge. "All right!" he said, in the way the school's advertising reads, Make a Film! Be Creative! Right On!

"How about a candle?"

J pondered it, imagining the treacherous path down from

Gerry's house to the school, descending it by candlelight.

"Do you have a light?"

"Light." Gerry did a little pirouette.

Ken, the 60-year-old maintenance coordinator with long, feathered hair looked up. "It's your turn to bid, Gerry. Jeez," he said, rolling his eyes.

The big, burly one with greasy jeans wordlessly held out his lighter.

"Thanks," said J.

Gerry dumped himself into the vinyl chair.

"Watch out for the cougars." the guy with the lighter added, as an afterthought.

"Yeah," agreed Gerry. "So, what was the bid?"

J is where he wants to be.

He walks the hill carefully, one foot in front of the other, negotiating the twisting, angular path one step at a time, feeling the rough ground with the whole of his foot before he shifts his weight forward. At every moment there is the chance that he will stumble, fall, tumble down head over heels until his head or face or back makes sudden, unforgiving impact against rock. He can't see what's on the path, or just below it, only the faint glow of light from the wilderness camp 400 feet directly underneath. He can hear the sound of teenagers laughing and performing for each other, indulging in the freedom of being on an island, separated from their parents by a thin segment of the Pacific Ocean. He wonders if they've realized they're not being supervised.

"I am not afraid!"

It's a boy's voice, the weird one, J thinks, the one with the Darth Vader sunglasses who pretends the world of interactive computer games is his own, inhabited and real.

"Ewww!" cries a female voice, maybe hers, he can't tell.

She is sixteen, just turned, according to the student breakdown sheet he checked surreptitiously after he led the getting-to-know-you, icebreaking exercise on the first night. It's the part of the week he likes most. Twenty or so city teenagers, strangers to each other and, in this new environment, to themselves as well, sit in a circle in the screening-room. Intimidated by their abrupt arrival into the woods, they slump protectively in their chairs. Skinny legs poke furtively out of cave-like pants, arms are folded across breasts and sardonic grins blaze brazen paths through frozen stares at the floor. J likes them like that.

One by one they go around the circle. He asks them to say two things. First it's something they want the group to know about themselves, then something they don't. If he can get them to admit something even slightly embarrassing about themselves they start to feel more comfortable with each other.

What she didn't want them to know was that her nickname at school was Martha Stewart. She giggled coyly when she admitted it, gawking self-consciously at the impenetrable blond snowboarder sitting next to her. Steve. Barely sixteen, freckled and seemingly pre-verbal, J disliked him on sight.

A large fern sweeps across his face unexpectedly, like the brush of fur, an animal he is semi-consciously expecting to pounce, or at least cross his path without warning to either of them. He crouches for a moment and catches his breath.

When he logs onto the internet he searches habitually for the sites which advertise young women, almost invariably pitched to the pornography consumer as "barely legal." Or "Little Lolitas." The one he visited earlier in the evening (remembering to deactivate the history folder which automatically keeps a record of all the sites the user has visited) tabulated his visit as the 762,899th since 5 July, two and a half weeks before.

He broached the subject earlier that night with Todd, the school's 22-year-old non-linear editing instructor. "It's natural," J told him, playing the experienced teacher unafraid to tackle difficult, shameful subjects. "Not a big deal at all."

They were talking about being attracted to their students, not pornography, though on the rare occasions that he tests the waters on that one, not with Todd or anyone he works with but with one or two of his close male friends, he is always met with a stuttered half-laugh and a stubborn refusal to pursue the conversation. J takes this as an acknowledgment of sorts, as evidence buried like pirate treasure, evidence that he is not alone.

She is like Martha Stewart, this sixteen-year-old girl with porcelain skin (from a distance, anyway, from across the room, from his vantage point, telescopic with desire). Her rapid, nervous gestures, a perky housewife in training, make it easy to imagine her skillfully managing a large and complicated household, arranging for sitters, preparing a flambé, matching wardrobe lacquers and the like. All this would be done with a subtle acknowledgment that she was not doing this for her own benefit but instead for those watching her—because, in his head, she is always being watched.

In the darkness, pausing to light another joint off the candle, he imagines that he is a camera, a steady-cam. In tight, she is cross-eyed. No, not cross-eyed exactly. The left eye wanders, aims itself at an angle across the eye-line established by the right. Inhaling, he imagines that this solitary flaw is what attracted him to her, but only because the eyes that never look in the same direction simultaneously are also stunningly, archetypically beautiful. Deep blue and speckled with fragments of black, like chipped ebony flakes.

That, and her ass, which like so many of the postpubescent girls he is attracted to, springs unexpectedly from her thin, boyish legs.

He thinks again that he can hear something rustling in the bushes, moving toward him. Gerry assured him that there are no predatory animals on this island. To get to Gramby they would have to swim eight clicks from the mainland, which, it is rumoured, they do, occasionally, though J suspects that this is a myth perpetrated by the locals to frighten city boys like him.

A gaunt kid with a shaved head and hollow eyes went next. His voice was flat and skeletal. "I don't have anything good to say about myself," he said. "What I don't want you to know is that I'm manic-depressive. And I'm on antipsychotics." He didn't look up when he spoke, except at the end, wrapping his mouth around *psychotic*.

Grasping at the sliver of eye contact the boy offered him, J took a deep breath. "Okay," he said carefully, masking the fear that wanted to creep into his voice. "Thanks."

I'm a good teacher, he reminds himself, buttressing the rising tide of his own darkness. He massages the floating voice in his head (what he loves most about pot) and lets himself remember: how, post-intro-exercise, he mustered the courage to tell the skeletal kid how brave he thought he was; the directness and honesty of his Day 2 pep talk. "I like to help solve problems," he tells them. "If you want to be left alone, just tell me to piss off; how they laugh when he says that and how they delight in telling him to piss off; that he let Sandra and Steve into the same group, against Todd's advice, because it's what they wanted; that he didn't dismiss their silly, cliché-ridden script (even for sixteen-year-olds); that he made the talented group happy by suggesting the lead character put the fish she was eating for dinner in the fishbowl; how, after Sandra had asked him for the second time what he thought of their script, he called a meeting.

"It's a natural reaction," he told them. "To look for approval. You worked for fourteen hours and wrote a script in

15

one day. But this isn't regular school. There are no As or Fs. What matters is what *you* think of the script. This whole thing is for *you*."

A branch snaps. He starts, then dismisses it as another of the lads' phantom cougars.

It is a constant craving. As young as fourteen or fifteen, never mid-stream pubescent but on the outer edge, where his dyke friend Kyra tells him his mother is trapped in her emotional development, still a little girl. He doesn't trust this diagnosis. It seems too easy, too pat and Freudian psychological; to pin this questionable if shared desire on his mother feels too much like blame. Blaming the victim.

After grinding the joint into the dirt, he blows out the candle. The flame's only tangible effect was to prevent his eyes from growing accustomed to the dark. And he's made it. He recognizes the large boulder looming at his right, which marks the beginning of the straightway which leads down to the school.

As he picks his way through the last stand of cedar stumps the light from the kitchen reveals her, with Steve the snowboarder, giggling again.

Unseen, J uses his pedagogical imperative to banish him into a creaky, under-inspected Gondola jammed with overweight skiers, imagines himself in Steve's place, watches himself enter her from be—no. Something else.

Her crystalline eyes looking at him and away at the same time.

At his knees, taking him in her mouth.

God. In these fantasies she is eager, even grateful (though no less efficient); like the *hornyyoungthings* on the net pretend to be, thoroughly titillated by the presence of a camcorder in their bathroom *(I just love being able to express myself!)*. He is penetrating her, sucking her youth and desire to please into him, holding it like a bubble, in his hands.

When she grabbed his arm after the acting on camera

workshop and asked if he thought she were good enough to get an agent, he said he would think about, do what he could. If she wasn't a child, he would have said it's about what we don't want other people to know; or the dark water running underneath.

Steve shrugs. He and Sandra amble down steps side by side but not touching.

J sits with his desire, wondering vaguely if he can get away with a couple of minutes to release the plugged feeling inside of him, pull the stopper from the dam. No, too sordid. Not right.

They are in the screening-room now, seven or eight of them, he figures, as his eyes become accustomed to the glare of the twenty-watt bulb, punctuated by flashes of the gangsta movie they are watching, in rapid flashes of blue and white. Were they laughing before he came in? Are they embarrassed by his presence? Through the dank heat of the room, he can see her massaging Steven's shoulders. It's a primitive back rub, all stiff-fingered staccato jabs, sharp sticks puncturing the surface of his muscly back. Steve watches the movie and betrays nothing for her, certainly not lust. J drinks the salty fear and loneliness he feels in this room. Losing perspective. Exhaustion and pot conspire with untenable desire and he silently draws a deep breath. Your erection is about you, he tells himself, not them.

Steve stands without warning, breaking off the massage. Sandra's hands float momentarily, stung and suspended. She glances quickly at the kids zombied around her then slides carefully back into her seat on the red, camel-back couch. He joins her and concentrates on the television.

What is his problem? J clears his throat. "Okay, guys," he says. "It's 11:30. I'm not going to force you to go to bed or anything but I ask you to remember how much work we did today. Breakfast is at 7:30 and we'll bang down your doors if we have to."

This self-consciously non-authoritarian advice hangs in the air for a moment while each teenager tries to read the reaction of the group before committing themselves. Slowly, Sandra extracts herself from the couch. She casts a prim, hopeful look toward Steve who doesn't notice. He's shooting a confidential glance at J.

"Good night," J says. "I'll see you guys in the morning."

From the bathroom near the linen closet, over the sound of his urine streaming into the toilet, he hears their rubbery footsteps on wooden planks, the click of trailer doors opening and the shudder of the wall when they're slammed shut.

But when he leaves, she's right there, at the cupboards, where they keep the extra blankets.

"Hey," he says casually, afraid his eyes are red. "Where's Steve?"

She wrinkles her nose. "He's working on the script."

"Hm. Doesn't strike me as the type."

"Do you know if I could get another duvet?" Her toes point toward each other, at cross-purposes, like her eyes.

"Sure, of course. We aim to please." He smiles, the light buzzing in his brain, a not-entirely unpleasant feeling, of being separate, outside of the consequences. His dyke friend Kyra, a fierce 50-year-old high-school teacher, admits to bursts of lust for the doe-eyed, downy ninth graders who, in improvisations she insists on participating in, have tenderly laid trusting heads on her bony, middle-aged scapula. And it's not like he's only attracted to barely post-pubescent girls, after all. Like the sun coming up tomorrow, 50 and menopause are close to Kyra, who treats him with love and respect. Who he'd sleep with in a second, if she were interested (and she might be).

Regrettably, Sandra's breasts are like peaches. Soft and

18

fuzzy and round.

She shifts her weight onto the outer edge of her left foot and looks at the ground. "I know you don't want me to ask this but do you really like our script?"

"Uh." His voice creaks, feels adolescent and shaky, like the squishy place that's being stimulated. "Yeah," he says, adding. "Well, it's a start, that's the important thing."

"You think it's stupid."

"No. I told you guys. First drafts, they're like that. Were you listening?"

She looks down.

"I, I think you're great. It's a pleasure to work with somebody like you."

He hands her a worn orange and brown duvet and a flowery pink blanket..

"They don't match. We're better at art than we are at bedding, I'm afraid."

She reaches out to take them.

I'm the adult here, he thinks and slowly, deliberately, leans forward, inch by inch until the tip of his nose brushes almost imperceptibly against her cheek.

She freezes.

He inhales the scent of her sweat mingled with girl deodorant, feels himself at fifteen, outside the secret smell of the girl's locker-room, b.o. recast as perspiration.

"And," he says, gently brushing the cheek with the back of his fingers, the down soft and deep enough to drown his hand. "You've got a mosquito on your cheek."

Through her tank top he can see that her left nipple is erect.

"You're great. That's what I think. And I should really go to bed."

Flakes of black looking in two directions simultaneously, liked chipped ebony suspended in an ocean of deep blue.

While he has one last look around the camp, hushed and expectant for the first time all evening, he remembers the story Kyra told him about being in Europe when she was sixteen. She rode the train from a small town in Germany (where her great-aunt was Physics Professor) all the way to Paris by herself. On the second night she lay in a crowded compartment next to another girl about the same age and peered through half-closed lids as a guilty-looking salesman in his thirties masturbated at them, his eyes darting back and forth between her and the girl beside.

In the editing suites in the basement below the screening-room he can just make out a faint sliver of blue light shafting through the blackness.

He walks over to the window, which has been carefully blocked with heavy black cloth and clears his throat.

There is a burst of activity from within.

He walks around the back to the basement door and pokes in his head. Steve emerges from the cubicle, closing the door rapidly behind him. Glancing down the boarder's body J sees a small stain seeping through the front of his thin cotton shorts.

"I was working on our script," Steve says.

"Oh, yeah."

"Yeah."

"Were you on the net?"

"No."

"Okay. Well, I'm not saying anything, just so you know, the internet's off limits to students, right Steve? Not because there's anything wrong with it, necessarily. Just because we have to be in control of what happens here."

"Sure." A jittery flood sweeps across Steve's body, which no longer seems to end at the boundary of his skin but jab out into the air between them, hot flashes and stinging nettles.

"Night, bud."

"Goodnight," Steve mumbles. Halfway up the stairs he turns. And smiles. "This is a cool place, man."

"Thanks," J replies, soaking up the gratitude, like a sponge.

He walks back up the hill in the dark, on all fours, one knee in front of the other, groping for the twists in the path and the exposed roots buried in the inky island blackness.

He tells himself that he didn't do anything wrong (fucking idiot that he is). That, if need be, he'll apologize. That it could be cast as a misunderstanding, which it must be, in some way.

In the house, the game is over. The table is littered with discarded beer cans and overflowing ashtrays. Gerry is propped up on the sofa-bed in the kitchen watching the news and scooping stabilized peanut butter from the jar with a stalk of celery.

"I got him," J says. "The little fucker was jerking off."

Gerry inhales through his teeth. "Hoooo, Wow!"

"Yeah, you should have seen him scramble."

"Yow! Ouch. Well, we all know a thing or two about that!"

J laughs. "Yeah. I just let him know it wasn't cool to be on the net. Maybe we should consider not giving out the password."

"Good. Excellent. It's good to have you here, man," Gerry says and toasts him with the flowery stalk.

The next morning she approaches him at breakfast, sans makeup and hair askew. He smiles and takes an adult sort of breath.

"How's it going?"

"I wrote something."

"Oh, yeah?"

"It's not the script, it's something else."

She hands him a single piece of lined paper with three holes, the type they make for kids to put in binders, to contain them, prevent them from getting crumpled and lost. This particular piece of paper is pristine, the writing is crisp and circular, frozen within its own arbitrary, even margins an inch or so from either end.

It isn't a rewrite of their film or even a screenplay or story or poem. It's just an idea, really, badly written and dismissable like so much of the personal writing he gets handed, fearfully and full of hope, by teenage girls over the course of a summer.

It's about a pretty, popular city girl who wakes up in the forest and discovers that she has transformed into a cougar. This cougar wakes up in a cave, her den, and feels movement beneath her. When she rises on all fours to nuzzle and examine her offspring, she sees that her children are not cougars, like herself, but people. All of them are boys or men, in perfectly realized miniature. Steve is one, cute and impassive. J is another, twitchy and fast, and so is Gerry, seven inches tall, unshaven and shirtless in an Andean print vest. And Todd, goofy and sexy and charming; and the weird kid who thinks computer games are real, or pretends to, anyway. In the story she huddles her furry length around them, for it is cold, and they nestle warmly into her dark, spiny fur, the snow-pack melting in a widening pool around them.

"Well," she says evenly. "What do you think?"

J doesn't know what to say. He doesn't know what to say because, watching her, as he has many times in the past 48 hours, he can't help but see: both her eyes are looking directly at him, perfectly aligned.

"I like it," she says, her feet buried solidly in the thawing ground. "It feels true."

More Like a Person (In My Country)

More like a person.

I'm on the bus and it's raining. It's the monotonous, Vancouver deluge; precipitation that you measure not in inches but months. It was last sunny for more than an afternoon a couple of months ago, more or less when I got my last gig, two days on a Movie of the Week called *Anatomy of Hell*. It was about a group of Libyan terrorists who hijack Red Cross buses and summarily execute the women and children cowering within. What they did with the (injured) men wasn't explained, though it was assuredly grisly and may very well have involved fucking them up the ass. I played Salim, the young terrorist with a conscience. I got a close-up, which was cool, except I kind of fucked it up. I had to crouch behind a jeep and point a 50-pound M-16 at the women and children about to be butchered in the foreground. This was when I was to have my moment of conscience. There was a representative from the Canadian army on set to verify weapons and personnel authenticity (though what he knew about Libyan terrorists was never explained). When we were setting up the shot he told me to crouch behind the jeep. The pressure on my less than developed quads hurt and my lower half began to shake. I asked the Army expert if I could hold the gun standing upright but he said, "No. Not realistic."

During the first take, the director ("Call me John," he said) noticed that I was shaking. He asked me if I was comfortable because it was an extreme close-up, in tight on the gun to my face. I told him I was fine. When my quads continued to vibrate John the director asked me again if I was okay, and I said, "Yes," even though I wasn't. John was an *artist*, though. He assumed my shaking was a product of nerves and forced the extras from Coquitlam in brown face

23

making ten bucks an hour to scream in fake Arabic while I trained my gunsight on them. "Watch them," John whispered just after he called action. "Feel the screams. Don't act, just *do it.*"

"Okay," I said, through gritted teeth. "I got you." After three or four takes he shook his head and said, "Okay, fine, that'll do."

At the Craft Services table, where they keep all the gourmet snacks the extras are forbidden to touch, John grabbed a double-chunk decadent-delight cookie and caught me eyeing him. "That was really good, you know," he said. "Well done."

"Thanks," I replied.

"You're welcome," he said, adding, "really. You were *great.*"

It was on TV last week, after Jeopardy. Because all the terrorists wore balaclavas, my grandmother in Bakersfield couldn't figure out which one was me. I missed it, because my partner and I choose not to have cable.

So I'm on the bus and it's raining and I'm on my way to my agent's, to pick up a script for an audition, my first in more weeks than I care to mention. The number 20 bus inches its way downtown from my hip lesbi-gay-latino artists' nook via Vancouver's approximation of the third world, the Downtown East Side. I'm going to pick up my audition script, though, so I'm slick and thick-skinned, like I've been coated with Vaseline. I am unfazed by the normally gut-wrenching cacophony of ravaged, stumbling bodies; of women in frayed mini-skirts and unkempt men I usually fear will lash out viciously at the slightest provocation.

Under normal circumstances, I'm not nearly so relaxed in close proximity to the drug-addled poor; a legacy, or holdover, I guess, from a time when I was on the tube in London, England, where I went to high school. Returning from an exhilarating performance of *Mother Courage and her Children* at the Barbican Theatre (winter home of the Royal Shakespeare Company) I found myself sitting opposite a fired-up trio of beer-soaked punks bent on removing all of the stuffing from their respective subway seats (one of them using his teeth). We were doing *A Clockwork Orange* in English 12 and I was entranced by this real-life embodiment of the rage I found so attractive in art. But the punk's ring-leader caught me watching them and leered at me and my overgrown mop of half-Egyptian curly hair.

"What are you looking at, fucking wanker," he demanded. I clutched my glossy 8x10 RSC program and looked at the floor. Even then, sequestered, virtual Yankee from the American School in London that I was, I knew: one privileged, Canadian-accented squeak and I would be dead.

Enjoying the surge of panic that had seized my zit-pocked body, the punk leaned across the narrow aisle until the tip of his nose was six or seven inches from my face. He was close enough that the smell of his clothes should have made me vomit. All my instinctive physiological functions were paralyzed, however, and I froze.

"I could rip your fucking head off right now," he whispered, hoarse and lippy. The commuter-packed car was hushed except for the sound of the subway's wheels clacketing slowly along the Victorian-era track. "Ponce, fag, wog," he sang throatily. "How 'bout I stick my cock in yer mouth?"

I shuddered.

"No? You don't like that? What about your ear then? Or your *nose*?" He stood up menacingly, jutted his left hip to the side and let his right wrist flop in front of him. I noticed his fingernails, which, unlike his hands, were curiously neat and manicured.

"I could put it up yer *nos*-tril," he suggested, making swivel motions with his hips, pretending what he assumed I was: poncy Eton boy, rich offspring of the Arabs who own Harrods and Crystal Palace. Dodi Fayed at fearful fifteen.

"I'm fucking gigantic," he said (about his penis). "But then I think yours'd almost be big enough to take it" (about my nose). "What do you think, wog boy?" He turned and smiled at his mates who were doing their dutiful best to enjoy his performance, despite their drunken stupor.

"Why don't you leave him alone," a nondescript young guy in a lime tracksuit suggested timidly.

"Why don't you *fuck off*," the punk responded. He turned to me and poured what was left of his tall can of McEwan's over my head and, after a good, tongue-clucking laugh about that, he and his mates left me alone.

"I was just kidding, cunt," he said before they hurled themselves off at the next stop. "*Cunt* you take a joke?"

On the Hastings bus however, in the *present*, I let it all slide harmlessly past me, opaque and inconsequential, even when a scruffy bug-eyed guy with sweaty cheekbones and the shakes stuffs himself in the vacant half-seat between me and an oversized balding man wearing polyester pants that don't quite reach his ankles. After wedging himself in next to me, the edgy guy turns and asks for a smoke. I smile and say, "Sure." When he lights it up with a quivering hand right there on the bus I suppress the impulse to feel guilty and choose instead to be grateful that I have been able to provide this suffering man with a moment of much needed pleasure. When he starts muttering to himself about the goddam Chinese (because the bus is almost entirely populated by *people of East-Asian descent*) I feel slightly more culpable. Wriggling my thighs free from his I head for the exit and make my escape.

"Thanks, man," the guy yells as I hop off the bus.

I smile, though he can't see because my back is to him. You see, as I mentioned, *I've got an audition.*

I walk the rest of the way to my agent Toller's office. Treading lightly across Cordova Street (the unofficial border dividing Vancouver's nouveau-riche from really-fucking-poor) I blinker past a couple of tourists trapped unwittingly on the cusp of this unmarked neutral zone, a green line, as it were, like in Beirut, where half my dad's family lives. There, it's to divide Christian from Muslim. My agent's office is in Gastown, where these tourists want to be. His building is sandwiched between two sets of newly erected luxury condominiums overlooking a brass-plated steam-clock. Because the clock is one of the city's few historical monuments it is featured in many an American Movie of the Week shot in Vancouver. There is a gaggle of Asian tourists gathered around it laughing and taking pictures. It toots cheerily as I pass. A sign, I figure, a harbinger of things to come.

In the faux marble lobby inside Toller's building, I watch the floor numbers decrease as the elevator descends from the top floor. I remember that when I went to pick up the audition script for *Anatomy of Hell*, I had to climb the fourteen flights of stairs to Toller's office because the elevators were being serviced. Actually, it's only thirteen flights but his floor is number 14 because 13 is, of course, bad luck. When I climbed those stairs, I *got* the part and for a moment I figure maybe that's what I should do now. For luck. Just in case. The elevator pauses at the fourth floor. Four is my favourite number. Maybe, I think, I should walk up to the fourth floor and catch the elevator *there.*

But then the second elevator's doors open, and who should amble out but the *other* 25-year-old brown actor Toller represents, Dez (or Daz, I can never remember). Toller always sends us out for the same parts and Dez (or Daz) usually gets them. He's better looking, East Indian—I think—sans hook nose, zits and manifest guilt about betraying his culture.

"Hey, Jason," Dez/Daz says, with a generous smile. "How's it going?"

"Hey...good," I say, electing not to risk one of his names. "What'd you get?"

"Oh, nothing much, just a *Hat Squad*."

"Oh, yeah?"

"You too?"

"Yeah," I say. "Stupid?"

"Very."

"Oh, well."

"Yeah."

I kick at the edge of the lobby carpet with my toe

"I had a couple of days on *Rumble in the Bronx*," he says.

I look up. "Oh, yeah?"

"Yeah. It was *very* cool."

"I bet."

"You seen it?"

"No, not yet."

"There's this scene where they put this guy through a tree shredder. You can see the mountains in the background. Since when are there mountains in the Bronx?" He laughs. "Funny, huh?"

"Yeah. Totally."

"You tomorrow?"

"Yeah."

"Well, maybe I'll see you there."

"Yeah," I say. "Maybe."

He strolls out of the building and I realize the elevator is rising again. I debate about whether or not to climb the stairs for a couple of minutes until the first elevator returns to the lobby. "Oh, well," I think. "It's easier to ride."

In the reception area of Toller's office, his secretary, Christine, is struggling to jam a piece of hole-punched computer paper into the ancient nine-dot-matrix printer they still use to print up our resumes. A large, horsey woman, Christine is an actor like me who works for Toller for the extra money. I like her. We *chat*.

"Hey, Christine."

Consumed with the printer, she doesn't look up. Every other half-decent agency (and despite appearances, Toller is a good agent, representing a number of excellent, visible actors) prints up their clients' work histories on a laser printer, or at least a bubble jet. I keep meaning to speak to them about this.

"Christine."

"What?"

"Uh, I'm here to see Toller."

"Oh."

"Is he busy?"

"I don't know. Why don't you ask *him?*"

Uh, oh, I think. This is Christine's fourth month at the agency. Toller's secretaries normally average just under three, because, I suspect, he's such an asshole to them.

"Toller," she calls flatly, still fiddling with the printer. "Jason wants to see you."

Toller pokes his head out of his office and runs his hand through the twelve strands of hair carefully arranged across his patchy red pate. He rechristened himself, officially, after Toller Cranston won the World Figure Skating Championships in 1978. He's got the little name-change notice you're required to post in a newspaper framed on his wall, next to a stark, black and white *No Apartheid Anywhere* poster. It's an abstracted black man, on his knees, screaming to the heavens. In the last election he also voted Reform. He made a point of telling me.

I smile. "Hi, Toller, sorry to bother you."

"No, no," he says, "come in."

"Thanks." I cross the threshold into his office pretending

the sort of relationship we ought to have (that of equals, colleagues). His clients' head shots are stored in metal baskets mounted on the rear wall of his office, a hundred or so faces peering out at us, threatening, eager, sardonic, seductive, ironic, earnest, hopeful—take your pick. Mine is at the top (A for Aba Moussa), to the left. I'm not smiling. Earnest.

"How are things?" I ask.

"Tolerable," he says. It's his little joke.

"Ha," I say, chuckling.

"How's the baby?"

"He's good. He's great," I say. "Although he's not really a baby anymore. They grow up so fast."

"Well, here they are," Toller says, turning to me and handing me the script. Four pages.

"Thanks."

He peers over the top of his bifocals. "Did you see Dez?"

"Yeah, yeah I did."

"You were lucky he got that Jackie Chan movie. The *Anatomy of Hell* people really wanted to use him. You were the second choice."

"Oh."

He drops his chin. "*What?*"

"Nothing."

"Well," he says, tapping his chin, now. "You're both up for this one, too. So you *better be good!*"

I nod.

"You know you have to do an accent."

"Oh, yeah?" I look at the sides. "What is he?"

"Oh, well, you know. *Whatever.*"

"Right."

"Seriously, though," he says. "Carol is very important."

She's the casting director. I've never auditioned for her before. She casts all the Cannell series shot in town.

"Okay."

"You've got to impress her."

"I'll do *my best.*"

"That's what I'm afraid of." He smiles. "Oh, *lighten up*, I'm just kidding. By the way," he adds, placing a hand on his hip. "Carol gushes. Don't let it throw you off."

"I won't."

"Don't blow it " he calls out again as I make my escape from his office. Knute Rockne, he ain't—despite any coincidental similarity in height. "Dez certainly won't."

On my way out, I elect not to say anything to Christine, who's still huddled behind the computer. As I reach for the door to the hall she looks up.

"If you think he's mean to you," she says, suddenly, "you should hear the things he says to me."

I smile weakly. I can't afford to get too involved, to say anything that might get back to Toller.

"Oh, yeah?"

"Yeah," she says. "Stupid, sardonic fag."

Toller appears at his doorway. She glances over her shoulder.

"Haven't you fixed it yet?" Toller asks.

"No, Toller, I haven't," she replies. "Maybe you should consider getting a half-decent printer."

He glowers and I don't say anything, either.

"Good luck with your audition," Christine says as I leave.

"Thanks," I say and just catch a glimpse of Toller hanging his head at his door, muttering something under his breath; something like, "He'll need it."

On the bus ride home I ignore the live action film strip of unrepressed despair framed by the bus' window and immerse myself in the *sides* (what we in the *biz* call the script you audition with). It's for the *Hat Squad*, another in an endless series of shows from Cannell, the schlock production machine that scored its first major hit with *The Love Boat*. It's what you'd call (in the *biz*) high concept:

31

three wise-cracking twenty-something brothers with swooshy hair, sons of a famous detective, form their own PI outfit and cleverly solve an endless series of grisly crimes, all the while wearing stylin' forties fedoras. Kind of like the Hardy Boys. For adults. Even Toller laughed on the phone when he told me about it. In this particular episode Stephen, Barney and Tad are hot on the tail of the notorious *Kissing Bandit*. A serial rapist with a sense of humour, the Kissing Bandit always leaves a signature white handkerchief after breaking into (good-looking) women's houses and raping them.

I'm auditioning for your standard TV immigrant Seven-Eleven clerk. Half pappadum-accent and half bumbling fanatic, this particular version mistakes Tad for the Kissing Bandit and tries to shoot him. According to an assistant director friend of mine, Tad is named for Stephen J. Cannell's corgi.

At a page and a half the scene is long enough to be a principal (more than 10 lines) which means I'll make $700 a day plus a 75% buy out (what they pay you for the right to broadcast it as many times as they want). Another 150 bucks for the costume fitting puts me at about 1200 bucks for five or six hours work. If we go into overtime (which happens maybe 25% of the time) I start making 130 an hour (plus buyout) on top of what I would already have been paid. Not bad work if you can get it.

My name is written in Toller's aggressively round print across the top. It's mis-spelled, as usual. Jason Ab*u*-Mouss*e*, it says, which I translate roughly to mean Jason, father of fluffy chocolate dessert. Ab*a* Mouss*a*, my real name, means son of Moussa, though I am not son of Moussa, I am son of Paul. Moussa was my grandfather, a doctor who killed himself after losing everything betting on Egyptian cotton futures in the fifties.

Cannell Productions
North Shore Studios
555 Brooksbank
North Vancouver, B.C.

All Talent Agents....
Scene 34.
For: Rahim, Corner-Store Clerk, 40's–50's. Ethnic,
accent, and a tad dim.
Please suggest: ANY non-white talent capable of
doing an accent.

33. (continued):

SHERI: I don't know...I'm so scared.

STEPHEN: Shhhhh. *(He touches her face.)* It's going to be
okay. I promise.

34. INT. — WEST SIDE CORNER STORE — NIGHT

*(TAD walks into a CORNER STORE and grabs a coke. The
CORNER STORE CLERK watches a SMALL TV underneath
his counter.)*

ANNOUNCER (VO): Police say the so-called Kissing
Bandit remains their number one target. He has so far
eluded a manhunt unprecedented in the history of
Chicago's police force.

(Tad approaches the counter.)

CLERK: Nice hat.

TAD: Thanks.

TV (VO): ...caution that the suspect is armed and dangerous.

TAD: How much?

CLERK: A dollar twenty-five.

(The clerk looks at the TV...)

TV ANNOUNCER (VO): ...and anyone seeing a person resembling this artist's rendition is asked to contact police at once.

(...and up at Tad.)

CLERK: Who do you think you are?

TAD: What do you mean?

CLERK: You disgust me.

(Pulls out a gun, points it shakily at Tad.)

TAD: Hey, pal. What are you doing?

CLERK: In my country, you would have your hands chopped right off, like *this*.

(Rahim karate-chops the counter.)

34

TAD: Look, Rahim, I'm telling you, you got the wrong guy.

CLERK: Don't talk! Don't move.

(*Rahim runs toward the door...*)

CLERK: Police, police! I've caught the kissing—

(*...and trips over the chip rack. Stephen sprints in, gun pulled.*)

STEPHEN: What's going on?

TAD: He thought he'd caught the kissing bandit.

STEPHEN: (*Laughing.*) You? I don't think so.

TAD: Well, you know, we *Caucasians* do all look alike.

It's the comic-relief segment, like the Porter in *Macbeth*, a moment of levity just prior the seatbelt scene (biz terminology, the point in the story at which the audience must fasten their metaphorical seatbelts because the plot is pulsating into overdrive). Though I'm not exactly 40 I figure I've still got a shot because, as an American casting director I did an audition workshop with said to me, "We have a hell of a time finding decent ethnic actors up here. If you can be there for the audition, you'll work. I guarantee it." The other morsel she offered to us novices (not just me, the ethnic) was, "To succeed in this business, you just have to be yourself."

That night I work on the text. Because I'm staying up late, I have to sleep in my son Seth's bed. My partner Jillian is an insomniac and me creeping into the bedroom late might wake her up. So I must sleep in the child's bed; become, for the sake of my work, the child. This, of course, is what acting requires: a childlike willingness to give yourself up to what you imagine others will want; abandoning whatever agenda or beliefs or depth you might hang your reasons for living on and diving naked into an unselfconscious, committed embodiment of what is described on the page.

It takes me about an hour to prepare. I...

—look at myself in the burgundy teak mirror from Indonesia I bought Jillian for her birthday and laugh at my face; my jaundiced brown skin, my giant hook nose, my acne scars, the big space between my teeth.

—tag the script line by line, making calculated, deft decisions about tone, attitude, stakes and prior circumstances.

—think about my Dad and the way he prostrates himself before all the old-moneyed white men at his country club.

—karate chop Seth's *Buzz Lightyear* action figure which is lying on my desk and imitate my aunt Souad, who, after 31 years of life in suburban Kansas City, still clings to her thick accent like a life-raft.

"*In my country, you would have your hand chopped off, LIKE THIS!*"

—whip around and pull a pretend gun on a picture of my Grandfather Aba Moussa wearing a fez.

"In *my* country, you would have your *hand* chopped off, like this!"

—imagine Rahim is my father, newly arrived from Cairo.

—remember Dad's funny immigrant story about his first night in *America*, when he called the operator and, in broken English, told her that he loved her.

"*In my country, you would have your hand chopped off, like THIS!*"

36

—think about the punks I met on the subway car and unremitting terror and place the emphasis on the last syllable, like an Arab.

"*Oo do you dink you AH?*"

—do the pappadum Seven-Eleven clerk from *The Simpsons*, for fun.

"*Dankyouberymuch.*"

—say to myself in the mirror, you can do it, buddy, you *can!*

—imagine Dez in miniature, two feet tall and whimpering in the corner of my study. "From the bottom of my heart, pal," I tell him. "You haven't got a chance."

—go through the scene seven times, without looking at the script once, doing all of Tad's lines in my head.

I *drop it in.* I *commit.* I pick out a costume and lay my photo and resumé carefully by the study door.

I masturbate. I go to bed.

Prepared.

At Lonsdale Quay the next afternoon I have to wait for fifteen minutes for the 236 Lynn Canyon, the bus that will usher me to the studio. I'm nattily clad in my generic ethnic immigrant costume: a worn, mostly polyester shirt with the top three buttons open and collar wings that reach my shoulders; generic khaki pants that don't quite reach my ankles; white sport socks; brown docksiders. My earnest ethnic 8x10 head shot and dot-matrix resumé are safely tucked away in the *Beautiful British Columbia* file-folder I always bring with me to auditions, for luck. Needless to say, it's still raining.

As I approach the stop I notice an old bum clutching your standard bottle of cheap booze in a paper bag worn smooth from too much tippling. He's staggering around the pole that marks my stop. There's nobody else around, just a diminutive Filipino-looking woman at the end of the bench. When I get close, the bum catches my eye and tosses me a toothy grin.

I smile back. Why not? I'm an actor, after all. And the marginalized deserve our attention. The bum squints for a second to ensure that he hasn't misread my reaction, then smiles again. He knows a sucker when he sees one.

Taking a deep breath, he begins to do vocal warm-up exercises.

"Meeee, meeee," he croons keeping a wavering eye cocked on me to assess my reaction. "Maaa, may, moooo."

I smile again.

He clears his throat. "Doncheeeettaaa laaa mooooooraaay," he sings holding his arms unsteadily in front of him. His voice is much richer and more accomplished than I expect as he sways over.

"Do you know who that is?" .

"No, I don't."

"Ah...then, do you know..." he says, pausing to let his body collapse on the seat beside me, "...who *Mario Lanza* is?" He enunciates this name with a gravelly resonance that suggests this person is his primary reason for getting up in the morning.

"Well, actually, I hang out at an Italian coffee bar on Commercial Drive. I think they very well might play Mario Lanza. It's the kind of stuff they're into."

"Oh," he says. "Then did you know that 30 years ago today, Mario Lanza sang Puccini, right here *in Vancouver?*" He pokes the bench repeatedly with his index finger.

"No," I reply. "No, I didn't."

"Aha!" he says, pulling himself up straight and bursting into a full-throated rendition of something Italian and unabashedly operatic.

It's not long before he gets winded, however, and stops. He takes a breath, pulls the right side of his dirty brown blazer across an exposed section of frayed, grey sweater and winks at me.

"Today is his birthday. Should I sing?"

"Sure," I say, affably. "Whatever you want."

His eyes narrow . He leans in close to me and jabs his index finger into his throat, just above his Adam's apple. "I went to McGill Music School," he whispers fiercely.

I breathe this in, keep my eye trained on his, so he'll know that I'm *hearing* him. "You did," I say quietly. "Wow."

"Yes," he confirms wearily, letting his chin tip back so that his head is resting on the top of the bench.

"From what I've heard that's a really good school."

He nods vaguely, then tilts his head sideways toward me. "You're a sensitive type, an artist," he tells me.

"Sort of," I say. "I'm an actor."

"Ohh, and you are going to the studio."

"That's right."

"What are you hoping to become?"

"Oh, it's stupid."

"What? Tell me."

"Well if you have to know, I'm auditioning for a 50-year-old Seven-Eleven clerk who catches the Kissing Bandit."

"The fuckers." He says it under his breath and gestures to the 236 stop marker, where an athletic young Hispanic man in a letter jacket is waiting for our bus. "People like him—they know nothing about *art*. Hey, *compadre*," the bum yells across to the Hispanic man. "*Comprende* Mario Lanza?" The guy looks at him for a second, and seeing it's a street person, pretends he didn't hear.

"*Muchos gracias, amigo*," the bum says, winking. After another brief burst of Mario, he slides down the bench toward the Filipino woman and stretches his arm carefully across the top of its backrest. His hand settles an inch or two from her shoulder.

"You are very beautiful," he whispers and I imagine the

39

hot stench of his rice-wine breath enveloping this woman.

She smiles and nods.

I turn away.

"I'm going to A&B Sound," the bum says, to both of us. "To buy a Mario Lanza compact disc, in celebration of *his birthday.*"

"Great," I say. "Good for you."

As if heralding the momentousness of this occasion, the bus pulls up and we all, Filipino, Hispanic, Arab and Street Person climb studiously aboard. Avoiding Mario's gaze, I walk determinedly to the rear section of the bus. I don't have to worry, though. The bum has to painstakingly count a dollar-fifty worth of nickels and pennies before the black bus driver in his late twenties will let him board the bus.

"You gonna be okay there, pal?" the driver asks.

"Oh, yes," the bum says. He drops the change, *en masse,* into the metallic coin receptacle. "My question is, *are you?*" Then he winks at him.

"All right, that's enough," the bus driver says. "Let's go." He jams on the accelerator and Mario pitches forward against the front window. After recovering himself, he asks, "Do you stop close to the A&B Sound?"

"Yeah, I do."

"That's where I'm going," the bum says. "To buy a compact disc. For Mario Lanza's—"

"Sit down, okay."

"Ah, yes. Of course. I will. Thank you," the bum says, bowing graciously.

On this route the bus goes fast. There are only a few stops, one at each of the malls and industrial centres spaced evenly at three or four kilometer intervals along the mountain highway. My stop is the tenth or eleventh, a fifteen- or twenty-minute ride. It's dark now and still raining.

Negotiating his way past an umbrella sticking an inch or two into the aisle, Mario spots a young Chinese girl in her

40

early twenties sitting near the rear exit doors. He lurches to an empty seat across from her.

"You are beautiful," he says. "I will sing for you."

Her eyes widen and she smiles involuntarily.

"I love to see a young lady smile," he says and bursts into a rehash of the Cornetto piece, though it's still disturbingly rich.

"All right, pal," the bus driver says, slamming on the brakes hard enough that the bus skids to a halt, pitching me forward against the vinyl seatback in front of me.

"This is your stop."

"It is?" Mario asks, surprised.

"Yep, this is it. Right here. A&B is just up the street."

I rub a little porthole of fog off the window next to my seat and see only this: trees stretching up on either side of the mountain; a stretch of shiny, slick asphalt that is the highway; a pair of headlights burning their way through the mist, coming up the hill toward us and then blinking abruptly out.

"Oh." Mario rises, confused, his Mediterranean bravado dissipating rapidly. The bus is silent, except for the sound of cars on the highway, and motionless, except for a couple who share knowing looks at Mario's expense. He makes his doubtful way back to the front of the bus, turns to the driver and asks, once again, "This my stop?"

The driver looks at him squarely. "Yup," he says. "This is it."

Mario grabs the metal pole in front of the exit and rotates himself to face us. Flashing a wide, conspiratorial smile, he announces, "Today is Mario Lanza's birthday and *I* am going to buy a compact disc. Shall I sing?"

Nobody responds, except for the bus driver. "All right pal, that's enough. I've taken you to your stop, now *get off*."

Mario nods and staggers down the three slip-resistant steps and steps onto the sodden gravel at the side of the highway. The doors close with a release of pressure behind him. The driver turns to face us. "That's better, eh?" he says, shaking his head.

I can just discern the vague outline of Mario's body through the fogged windows on the other side of the bus. He's turning his whole body 180 degrees, back and forth, searching for the A&B sign, something titanic and neon, a beacon. As we pull away, I twist myself around to see if I can make him out through the back of the bus but I can't.

Approaching the studio at a trot, my heart begins to pound. Nerves. My first real bout. It's fine, I tell myself, no big deal.

There's something unquestionably military about the place: the little divided Berlin guard post at the entrance to the studio, the ten-storey sound stages looming in the background, like airplane hangers.

It takes me twenty minutes to negotiate my way into the casting-room, following the laser-printed signs protected from the air-conditioning by thick plastic sleeves. "HAT SQUAD AUDITIONS ⇒" they proclaim. Then ⇑, and ⇐, through a maze of pink pastel corridors and polished cement staircases.

Judging by skin colour, there are two Rahims in the casting area already. When I walk in one of them is sweating and poring over his script so I know I don't have to worry about him. The other Rahim is Dez.

"Hey, man," I say, picking up the sign-in sheet, but Dez doesn't hear me. He's talking animatedly with a determinedly perky blonde wearing stiletto heels and a hot-pink mini-skirt. She must be out for the prostitute for the Kissing Bandit murders.

Hearing the nervous Rahim mumble, "In my country…" I look over just long enough to catch him giving his 8x10 an inadvertent little karate-chop with his hand.

"It's crazy," Dez says. "When they were chasing him through the streets, you can see a seaplane taking off in the background. Since when are there seaplanes in *the Bronx?*"

I close my eyes and smile. Definitely a good sign. I got my first film and TV gig when the director of a feature called *Intersection* saw a song-and-dance kid's show I was performing on Granville Island. He thought we'd be pretty great to have in the background of a scene where an adulterous father (Richard Gere) takes his suffering child for lunch. After watching us perform the show the director waxed eloquent while patting his foot-diameter paunch. "You know," he said, sweeping his arm out across False Creek toward the condos on the north shore. "With the mountains and this island, this city is *magnificent*." He paused thoughtfully. "In this picture we're not going to pretend it's in the States. We're just gonna to call it *Vancouver*. And," he added, "I don't give a shit what the producers say."

"That's great," I stammered. And it was. I was thrilled.

"I played one of the punks," Dez is telling the actress with feathered hair. He's leaned closer now, hitting on her. "I wore this stupid leather jacket with holes around the nipples."

"Eww."

"Oh, I don't know. I smashed a beer bottle and told Jackie Chan to get stuffed."

"That's cool," she says.

"Yeah, it was," Dez says modestly. "But he was a really nice guy. And you know what, he does all his stunts *himself*."

Casting Director Carol Kelsall swings her office door open assertively, releasing a 50-year-old East Indian man with stubble and a stoop. We all look up. She glances at her sheet, peers at us for a second and says, "Jason?"

I hold up my hand.

In one breath, she power-walks the seven or eight steps between us and places a stiff hand an inch or two from my face. "Hi there," she says. "I've heard *terrific* things about your work."

I try to thank her but I'm too slow.

"I'm Carol Kelsall," she continues. *"But you know that!"* She opens her mouth long enough to indicate a laugh. "So why don't we get straight to it? Follow me."

I do.

"Wow," she says, when she's closed the door to her office. "You went to the *National Theatre School.*"

"That's right." I smile, to be ingratiating.

She runs her pen down my resumé. "And you were on *Anatomy of Hell.*"

"Yeah, I was."

"Who did you play?"

"Uh, Salim."

"Good for you."

"Thanks."

"What else have you been up to?"

"Well, I had a kid a couple of years ago, I've spent a fair bit of time looking after him. And I'm teaching a lot."

"Oh, that's great," she says. "Wonderful. Mine is five and a half."

"Oh, wow. They're something else."

"Aren't they?"

"Yeah, they certainly are. Changes everything."

"It *sure does.*"

"Well," she says, dropping the smile like it never existed. "Let's see what you can do. Ready?"

"Absolutely."

"Good. Jamie, the director, couldn't be here," she says, pressing the record button on a video camera next to her. "He's shooting in LA so we're putting everything on tape. Slate first, please."

44

I take a breath, then address the camera with studied nonchalance. "Hi. My name is Jason Aba-Moussa and I'm with Northern Stars talent."

Carol nods. I settle on the image of my father prostrating himself to rich white men and begin to watch an imaginary TV. She fixes me with a steely, Chicago cop gaze.

I look up. "Nice k-hat," I say. *Suspicious*.

"Thanks," she reads. *Like she gets it all the time.*

She gestures a Coke bottle onto a non-existent counter.

"How much?" she asks. *Casual*.

"Dullar twenty-five." *Happy to make the sale.*

"The kissing bandit, blah blah, blah," she says, dropping the cop for a moment, to indicate the television-news report.

I do a double-take, put two and two together. It's him, I think to myself. It's the *Kissing Bandit*.

"Who du you think you *aah*?" I ask.

"What do you mean?"

"Eeen *my* khountry—" I start to say it, full of righteous, comic venom...then I don't know what happens. I don't think about Mario Lanza or the punks on the subway in England (though, this is what, more than anything, this event feels like). I don't think about the Gulf War, or my cousin John, one of only eight Allied Arabs killed in it (by Americans, by friendly fire). I don't think about anything except what I'm doing, which is trying to get this part, a part I want, desperately. I don't think about this woman in front of me, whether her gushing is an accurate reflection of who she really is or wonder if she is capable of tenderness (though, if I did, I would doubtless say yes, of course). I don't imagine her putting her child to bed, much like I do mine, with structured layers of awe and loathing, I don't wonder if she ever takes the bus to work or cares about the people she auditions, I don't wonder if she's been raped or if even if she ever considers that her husband might very well visit prostitutes.

There's no grand justification, really. Just wanting it too much is all I could probably be accused of; stupid, amateurish need. Validation. I get confused, I guess. Or maybe it's because I got the omens wrong, the wrong combination of stair climbing, bum talking and bus-taking made it astrologically impossible for me to get the part. Whatever the *reason*, I don't know how truly awful I am, bug-eyed and waving my hand like it's a gun, Yosemite Sam on Benzedrine; not until I stop and I realize I'm panting, that my palms are wet and I can feel my heartbeat in my fingers.

Astonished by my own peripateia, I gulp in some air and nod at Carol, to let her know that I'm done. She looks at me for a long moment, tapping the end of her nose with her pen, then says, "That's great Jason, very good. I want to go through it again. Only this time," she adds, leaning toward me ever-so-slightly. "This time, could you do it more like a person?"

More like a person.

Two days later the phone rings and I know it's Toller so I don't answer it. The answering machine picks it up.

"Well, Jason," he says, "Good news—"

I leap over Seth's Caterpillar buggy to grab the phone. "Hello, Toller? Just a second!" Because our answering-machine is a cassette-consuming relic from a pre-digital age the only tangible result I get from pressing the stop button is a burst of ear-shattering feedback.

"*God, what is going on?*" he demands.

"Just a second," I shout. I hit the button again and the whine stops, but for some reason we're still being recorded and there's an echo, like when I used to call North America from England.

"Ja-son?!"

"Hi. Sorry, Toller."

46

"You need a new answering-machine! What if it breaks down when I need to contact you?"

"Yeah, I know. We're going to get voice-mail, I think."

"Uh-huh. *Well*, you got the part."

My heart pounds with (what?) the momentary illusion that *I matter*, that I am *the one*.

"To be honest," I say, "I didn't think I was, you know, all that great."

"*Well*," Toller says. "Carol said you were *awful*. She wasn't even going to put you on the tape but when the director saw it, I don't know. *Apparently* he liked you. She said he wanted someone who looked desperate because *that's what it's like* for those immigrants. They're *desperate people*." He laughs. "I told Carol, anytime you want someone desperate and ethnic, Jason Abu-Moussa is your man."

I don't correct him, though it's Aba-Moussa.

"So. I'll courier the blue pages over to you when I get them. You shoot on Thursday."

"Thanks, Toller."

"Don't thank me. *I* didn't do anything. By the way," he adds. "I let Christine go, so I'll be on my own here for a week or so. So don't call unless you have to."

"Oh. Well, um. That's too bad."

"She wasn't working out."

"Yeah, um—"

"*Bye!*"

And all is well. Okay?

Adultery! Dysfunction! Trauma!

Things That Made Me Weird, Then:
1. I didn't have a girlfriend.
2. My nose was too big.
3. I had big, pus-filled zits on my face and back.
4. My big, painful pus-filled zits were unpoppable (believe me, I tried).
5. I thought I liked my parents.
6. I went to boarding-school.
7. I despised Led Zeppelin.
8. I was pathologically insecure.

Mom was coming back the next night. She was on a three-week Somatic Experiencing Bodywork Retreat in California, to get some space. And while she was gone Dad hadn't come home once before eleven. She already knew. Before she left she told me. It wasn't exactly a secret.

Twenty to twelve, Kari'd left an hour ago, my best friend's girlfriend. I was sitting on the couch reading the paper and I decided I was going talk to him. I had to, right. I mean, I knew it was weird to say shit like that to your parents but they always said to me, We don't hide things in this family. If you have something to talk about, just *say it*. So that's what I was going to do.

I heard Dad's key in the lock. He was humming, an off-key mutilation of *Three Blind Mice*. Bad news. "Jason?" he sang out. "Are you still up?"

"I'm in the living-room." I yelled.

"See how be-bum," he crooned. "Hee how be-bum."

Sauntering into the dining-room overlooking Mom's garden, Dad loosened his tie with the Mexican sombreros on it and asked if I wanted a beer. I smiled. "Sure." My parents were cool that way.

"How was your night?" Dad asked, ambling toward the bar.

"Pretty good," I told him. As I ran my hands across the lines of the corduroy slip-cover Mom made to protect the couch my fingers remembered the furrows ironed deep into Kari's thigh.

"I thought you'd have a good night," he said. "That, Kari, she's a *looker*."

He knows, I thought. He knows everything. He even knows how far I got, *almost all the way*.

Dad always gave me the old nudge-nudge, wink-wink if it was even hinted that I might have spent more than a few minutes talking to a girl. It started when I was four, with a gang of six- and seven-year-olds who played baby with me in our high-rise courtyard. In my *Wee Me* baby book there's a picture of the five of us, four *females* and me, sitting on a stone wall in an orderly line, our hands crossed solemnly across our laps, the North Toronto pre-Evangelical Calculus Club. Whenever we look at the picture Dad gets all man-o, man-o, says, "Remember them Jason, ha, ha, ha. Ooh, boy, I wish I could have been four years old with *them*." Because Dad's really good looking, he can get away with that kind of thing.

"Uh, look Dad, I've got something I want to say to you," I said.

"Oh you do, do you?," he replied, tossing me a wink. He wanted me to tell him that I lost my virginity. Or, more to the point, he was worried that I hadn't.

Toting a Coors Light and three fingersfull of Canadian Club to the table, he sat down. "So, Jason, what's the big news?"

It spilled, no—spurted, no, *puked* out of me.

"Look, I don't want to know, okay? I don't want you to say anything to me about it because it's none of my business. I just, well, it's—I know that Mom thinks you're having an affair. She told me—I'm sorry. But like I said, I don't care, I couldn't care less. All I'm trying to say is I think you should talk to her about it, tell her the truth. Either way. Because that's the only way that things are going to get better—that's what you guys always say, right? That's the only way people can figure stuff out."

He held up his hand, "Jason, whoa, son. It's okay. Just calm down."

"I know," I said poking my pinkie finger absently into a small hole in the checkered tablecloth. "I *am* calm, Dad."

"I know you are," he said.

"Sorry."

He stared at me for a moment.

"First thing, Jason. I just want to tell you, I have never—"

"Uh, like I said," I interrupted him. "I don't want you to tell me anything. I don't want to know. I just think you should talk to Mom."

"Let me finish."

"Sorry."

"That's okay. I *want* you to know. And this is what I've said to your mother, I don't know how many times." He took a careful breath. "I am not nor have I ever had—an affair. We are having some problems, it's true. She," he said, inhaling again. "She takes everything so seriously. So she's having some problems adjusting to life back here, in Toronto—that's not unusual after you move halfway across the world. But you know what she's like. What she thinks —you have my categorical assurance—it is absolutely and totally untrue."

"Okay, Dad, okay. I'm sorry."

"It's all right." He leaned back into his chair and swirled his scotch carefully in the dark. "Nothing to be sorry about. Your mother is very sensitive right now. It's all that spiritual stuff she's gotten into...."

50

"Okay."

"Are you all right?"

"Sure," I said, draining my beer, getting up to go upstairs and watch TV.

"Good. I'm glad we talked. It's important to talk about things."

Talk. Ha! I say. Ha! and Ha! again.

It's the thin film that separates us from our parents. They fuck us up, we all know that. My question is: does it ever go the other way? Do *we* fuck *them* up?

My mom would say so. Or imply it, anyway. She'd never come out and say it, like, "Jason, my son, he's cold and ungrateful," because she knows it's more complicated than that. But she would tell you about the time I was ten when, trying to keep up with a group of teenage boys, I braked too quickly going down a ravine and was catapulted over the front of my bicycle. I knocked out two thirds of my left front tooth and gashed open an inch and a half chunk of my lip. When Mom tried to comfort me—while my father watched from the front step—I turned on her. Spitting teeth and blood, batting at her breasts with my fists, I screamed, *"Leave me alone!"* And, when she didn't, *"Fucking bitch!"*

If you're a mother, that fucks you up. She's come over to ask for a bit of help, that's all. I know that. I *understand*.

But I have a child now, a partner and a child, a sort-of career, a qualified life. And a broken tooth does not constitute *trauma*.

She's working on a letter to send out to lawyers, to try to drum up clients for her practice. She's a therapist now. It's her great act of personal revenge against the social structure that gave her a masters degree then demanded that she shut her mouth and keep the house tidy. After fifteen or twenty

51

years she began to stand on her head and go to Gurdjieff groups. Then she refused to let Dad's boss smoke when he and his wife came for the bi-annual, bring-out-the-bone-china-for-the-dude-with-the-power schmoozorama. Actually, she didn't refuse. She told him to go ahead and smoke *that cigarette.* After Mr. Pattison lit up—with some apprehension, it should be noted—Mom casually and systematically opened every window in the house. In Toronto. In January. That fight lasted a week. Over the next year or two, Dad's affairs became progressively less secretive and then she got unceremoniously dumped.

So now Mom's a therapist. A *family* therapist. Trouble is, she doesn't have many clients, mostly the therapy-illiterate who chance on her self-effacing photo-ad in the Yellow Pages. But she won't give up. With seven years of post-divorce, post-secondary training in a bevy of therapeutic disciplines under her belt, she had planned to be making a hundred grand a year by now.

Her most recently concocted recipe for success is to contact every injury lawyer in the phone-book who might have a client experiencing the symptoms of trauma. To them she will pitch her hard-earned expertise, hoping the lawyer-type will refer clients to her practice. She worked it all out with her therapist. Trouble is, this kind of naked self-promotion makes my mother crazy. It takes her to *that place,* her lost little girl place, her *trauma* (and, as she says, she *knows* about trauma).

Barging into our Asher painting of an apartment uninvited ("The door was open!") she dumps her Mountain Equipment Co-op backpacks full of extra sweatshirts, emergency raingear and Q-tips on our kitchen table and asks me to help with the letter; to *react* to it, *shape* it; to be her *editor.* To which—catching the rising scent of my well rehearsed and as of yet untapped fury (a jellyfish, I think maniacally, she's like a fucking jelly fish)—she adds, "Is this a bad time?"

"No, Mom."

"Oh," she says. "Are you sure? Because I can leave."

"It's fine. But I can't help you with the letter," I add. "I'm really busy. Maybe some other time."

Okay. Context time. Because I know what you're thinking. Don't be a jerk, just help out your mother. Today, it's a letter. Two months ago, it was brochures. Dozens of brochures. Different designs, layouts, seven varieties of paper. Once, twice a week, she arrived at our place, clutching them like rosary beads, asking for *feedback*. A typical conversation:

(Mom holds up one of seven brochures with a hand-drawn, swirling, three-pronged rolling-ocean-wave picture on it.)

MOM: So what do you get when you look at this one?

ME: Um, well to be honest, I'm not sure.

MOM: I see. *(Pause.)* What does it make you feel?

ME: I don't know.

MOM: Okay. How do you mean?

ME: What?

MOM: What aren't you sure about?

ME: Sorry?

MOM: Something sets you off, makes you unclear. Can you tell me what it is?

ME: Well, the swirly thing looks kind of hand-drawn.

MOM: What's wrong with that?

ME: Nothing.

MOM: You don't like it?

ME: I didn't say that. It just, to me, looks kind of tacky.

MOM: *You* think so.

ME: Well, yeah. I mean, in my opinion.

MOM: Oh. *(A long pause.)* It's to give a sense of authen-

53

ticity.

ME: Okay.

MOM: But it doesn't work for you.

ME: Not really. But that's just me.

MOM: I see.

ME: Mom, you asked me what I thought and I told you, that's all!

MOM: Hmmmmm. Yes, I understand that this is difficult for you.

And so on. A month before that it was the ads: Should I do *Common Ground*, Yellow Pages, or *Therapist Monthly*? Picture or no picture? Hypnotherapy or Abuse Issues, which should go first? I've had enough.

But after my refusal, Mom breaks the rules. Removing her carefully preserved Albert Einstein sweatshirt ("It's really hot in here," she says, giggle-critically) she mentions it. Him. Not only that, but she equates us. She shouldn't do that.

"Sometimes being with you," she announces, "is just like it was with your father." This rare moment of direct confrontation about the past instantaneously transforms me into a twitching mass of adolescent rage and guilt. A trigger, she'd call it. I clench my fists and stare at the floor. Avoid her grey-green, squinted eyes, I tell myself, because they *swallow you up*.

"It's true," she says, defensively. "And I'm not afraid of the truth."

I chew at a hardened bit of cuticle under my fist-clenched thumb, feel it lift, scab-like, taste the blood oozing happily from underneath.

"Whenever I showed weakness," she continues, "you and Paul hammered me down."

Bursting, I pitch forward and pull at one of my socks, hard enough so that the seam between the knit tube and the plainly stitched foot-bit at the end begins to tear.

"Ahhhhhh!" I yelp, quivering, trying to stifle it, the *what* —morass—see myself in long shot from the ceiling and think, a grown man, flailing at his sock, primal-screaming at his alone-in-the-world mother with inverted nipples. How *impressive*.

She laughs, a spastic, involuntary hiccup of a laugh. The sock rips almost in half.

All right, I tell myself, *calm down*. In an unanticipated moment of rationality, I inhale deeply through my nose.

"Ahhhhhh," I say, exhaling.

"Hahahhahah," she titters, holding her breath.

We sit like this for a moment, Mom and I. The fridge hums happily behind us. Outside, our drunken 30-something post-punk secretarial worker neighbours yell at each other for more beer.

"Are you okay?" Mom asks.

"I can't talk about this right now," I say. "It's too *nuts*." In an unpremeditated bit of vengefulness, I hit the last word so she'll know what I mean, *who* I think is crazy.

"For you," Mom says. "It's too nuts *for you*."

"Right," I concede, pursing my lips apologetically. "Yes. Quite right. It's too nuts *for me*."

I tap my now partially exposed foot in time to the thrash-metal bass pounding through our kitchen floor. Mom fingers one of the many water stains on the dinner table she gave Jillian and me, three months ago, *in perfect condition*.

"You could get this sanded down," she offers.

"What?"

"The table. You could get someone to sand it down. To get rid of the stains."

I clench my jaw. "I'm sorry we got stains on your table. Okay?"

"Whenever I try to show empathy," she says, starting to cry, "you just push me away."

55

I'm not a total asshole, okay? I can imagine Mom's side of things. I think.

It haunts her, this ordinary web of anguish between us. It's taken up residence. The dreams are the hardest. Every day she wakes herself up at 4:30 in the morning, to meditate, she says but I know better. I think she rises two hours before dawn so there will be time to shake off her dreams before it gets light. It's better if they seep out in the dark, as if dread can be seen. What walks carefully into the surrendering night is an image of herself, opaque and blurred with failing eyesight. A middle-aged woman, abandoned by her husband for his secretary, forced at 51 to conjure, instantaneously, a life. From what the world deems nothing. From 30 years of doing as she was told; from every year-and-a-half a new suburb, new friends, a new *life*; from chocolate-chip cookies bought from that really excellent orchard place that takes 45 minutes to drive to but it's worth it because they're for my husband, my boy, my *family* (and, truthfully, I don't have a hell of a lot else to do). From this she must squeeze a career, a job, some hope.

Why women of my mother's generation and social status claw at their adult children: *we are all they had.*

Or so I imagine.

Whenever I try to show empathy, you just push me away.
Whenever I showed weakness, you two just hammered me down.

They cling to me, these words. They're up my nose, on my skin, suffocating me. Like the faint smell of the sweatshirt she forgets at our place, leaves hanging on the wicker chair after our little *why won't you help me with my letter* sockripping incident. It chokes me, the vaguely Vicks-Vapo-Rub scent of my mother's embrace—

I can't bring myself to touch it. All the next day, it lies there, growling, daring me to come near. Finally, as my partner Jillian seems disinclined to deal with it, I decide to fold it and put it away. Unable to resist burying my face in it, however, I resolve in a pique of self-conscious determination to march it straight out to the balcony and burn it.

It takes a while to get going but after I squirt it with several shots of our barbecue fluid, it makes a pretty good flame. Unfortunately I have to leave it smoldering on the porch when my six-month-old son Seth wakes up early from his nap.

Within hours, several members of our 25-suite Co-op complain to the board chairperson about the smoke. There is an emergency meeting, first of the maintenance committee and then, after a referral to the board for a jurisdictional directive—there being some question as to where responsibility for a possibly inappropriate burning of clothing on a private balcony lies—to the membership committee. After agreeing not to burn anything on the balcony (because of fire codes and the like) without written permission from the membership committee (with whom, it is decided, full authority rests) I try to make a joke.

"Really," I tell the committee chair. "It could have been a lot worse. I could have tried to burn *my mother* on the balcony. Now *that* would have been something."

She just nods, warily. The threat of matricide, no matter how off the cuff its telling, rarely strikes politicized 50-year-old women as humorous.

So, feeling guilty, I call Mom. I tell her, fine, I'll edit your letter, no problemo. She's thrilled. All is forgiven.

Things That Make Me Weird, Now:
1. I obsess about my parents—like my mother.
2. I have a kid.
3. I never go out.
4. I'm not successful enough.
5. I have a kid.
6. I'm mean—like my father.

7. I teach acting classes to ten-year-olds in community centres.
8. I'm addicted to visual and aural depictions of people having sex.
9. I have a kid
10. I can't let go of the past.

Mom cooked chicken for dinner the night she got home from her retreat, the summer before my parent's *separation*. Dad's favourite. He liked the bones, the dark meat, chewed up the whole bird, bones and all. Like an animal, my mother always joked. In three weeks I'd be back in boarding-school, 200 miles away.

Halfway through dinner, Mom announced, vibrating, that she had had a *significant experience* on her retreat, one she felt compelled to share.

"Go ahead," instructed my father, crunching down audibly on a plasticky joint-tendon thingy at the end of a tibia.

"Well," she said. "One night I passed a car parked where we were all staying. Inside I could see a couple, a *lesbian* couple, hugging."

Whoa, I thought, *Weird*.

"And making out," she added, looking at me. "The next day when we were doing our morning check-in, I don't know, it had really upset me, so I felt like I had to say something about it. I told everybody, including the couple—they were in the workshop. I said, 'I found that very disturbing. I don't like it when women are, like that, with each other.'"

"Hmm," agreed Dad, wiping grease off his fingers onto a paper napkin.

"But after we talked about my feelings and did some work on the table, I realized, it wasn't the lesbianism I was upset with."

The way she said *lesbianism* made me think of Kari, of my best friend's girlfriend, of my almost first time.

"Oh," asked Dad, interested.

Mom paused for a breath. "It was the sight of two people being intimate," she said finally. "I'm not used to that." Dad looked up from his wing.

And I saw the whatever remained of the thin silvery line of thread between them snap.

Mom's lawyer letter is in my mailbox the next afternoon, after I get back from teaching at the Boys' & Girls' Club. There's a friendly, handwritten *post-it* note attached.

Dear Jason,
Thanks so much for doing this. I *really* appreciate it. Any and all feedback is welcome. P.S. If you're willing, I could also use some help rehearsing the phone calls to the lawyers. I've got seven or eight possible scenarios. If you could pretend to be their secretaries I want to practice convincing them to put me through.
Love,
Mom (Jo) (Grandma)

I open the envelope and read.

894 W. 23rd Avenue
Vancouver, V6N 1B5
(604) 875-9870   Jo Harriman, MA, R.C.C.

Date

Dear Legal Professional,

Every day you meet with clients experiencing the stress of trauma in their lives. I am a therapist specifically trained to help your client move through the debilitating effects of traumatic events. Your trauma-tized client loses normal flexibility to respond to many ordinary life situations. They remain frozen in the memory of the accident, the threat, the attack, loss, etc. Your client is stuck in this place of psychological and physiological incompletion.

Debilitated, I skip to the end.

Enclosed are three brochures that explain more about what I do and something about how I do it.
I will call your office during the coming week to arrange a brief meeting with you. If you have any questions, please don't hesitate to call me at (604) 875-9870. I look forward to meeting with you soon.

Yours truly,

Jo Harriman

After kicking a hole in our back porch's common wall, I briefly consider burning the letter. Having given my word of honour to my co-op comrades, however, I reconsider and instead tear it into tiny, irretrievable shreds which I toss vengefully into our kitchen sink garbage.

"Well," Mom says when I call to tell her I just can't handle helping her out right now. "I guess I should go then."

"Okay," I say. "Sorry."

"That's fine. I'm sure I'll find a way through. Oh, by the way," she adds. "I think I might have left a sweatshirt here last week. Have you or Jillian seen one?"

"No, I haven't. Are you sure it was here?"

"Oh, well, I'm just, I think I had it when we talked." Her voice trails off momentarily. "I think it's the purple one, with Einstein on the front."

Great spirits have always encountered opposition from small minds.

"If it turns up, I'll let you know."

"Maybe I should ask Jillian if she's seen it."

"Okay, Mom, I *will.*"

She explodes. "You can't blame all this on *me,*" she cries. "Do you remember what he called you, that time in New Jersey when you went over your bike, when you were in so much pain?"

"No," I say, shutting her out.

"Ugly, awful names," she says vaguely, battling something unseen, on the periphery.

"Oh. I see."

Silence.

She says it quietly, bitterness blunted by the simple statement of fact. "He left, you know. Not me."

Year my Parents Separated: 1985.

Year my Parents Divorced: 1987.

Length of my Parents' Marriage: 23 Years

Amount of Money they Spent on Lawyers and Court Fees during their Divorce Proceedings: $40,000 (est.).

Number of Adulterous Affairs Conducted by my Father, 1964-1987: In excess of five (if you believe my mother).

Number of Adulterous Affairs Conducted by my Mother, 1964-1987: Two (if you believe my mother).

Number of Adulterous Affairs Conducted by Me in my Current (and Only) Cohabiting Partnership, 1989-1997: One (if you believe me).

After dinner we sat in silence. They sipped their mugs of hot water (three months before Dad had banished caffeine from the premises). I listened to the Atkins barbecuing hamburgers on their porch next door.

Smiling, Mom told us she wanted to do an exercise. "It's the checking-in round we did on the retreat," she said. "What we'll do is go around the table one at a time and tell each other whatever comes to our minds."

"Okay?" she asked Dad.

"Sure," he said. "Why not?"

"And I'd like us to hold hands."

"All right," he agreed, proffering both hands across our scraps of wings, cabbage and nuts.

Mom took his hand gratefully. It was the first time I'd seen them touch since she got back.

His other hand floated above my plate. I looked at it.

"Go on, Jason," he said. "Let's do this. For your mother." It was the controlled voice, trying to do the right thing. Though I did as I was told, I shook. My father gripped my palm and through his skin I felt him say, I love you, despite everything, all this, I do.

"Jason?" On my left Mom was holding her hand out, too. Reluctantly, full of ick, I took it.

"Now," she said. "The first thing we do is breathe together. In..."

We watched her. Letting her lids fall halfway across her eyes, Mom gazed out into some promising future of marital and filial bliss and inhaled loudly through her nose. I glanced at Dad.

"...and out." Dad did it now. I followed along.

"Hmmm," Mom concluded. "That felt good. It's important to centre."

"Yes," agreed my father. "It is."

I snuck a look at the kitchen clock. 7:23. Seven minutes until *M*A*S*H*.

"Now what we do is go in a circle and each of just says the first thing that comes to their mind about each other. What's really there for us in the moment. In *this* moment.

It's a way of making contact, of building bridges." She looked at Dad meaningfully. He held her gaze without giving an inch. She winced, then suggested that Dad should start.

"I'd be happy to," he said, looking at each of us in turn, smiling at me. "I'm just really glad to be here. And this—" he reached for the word, "*exercise* feels very good, very.... It's important to be together. To talk."

"What do you want to talk about?" Mom asked.

"Uh, well. I'm just. Very happy to be here with you both. My family," he said. On the last word his voice caught and through his left hand I felt a faint shudder. Three minutes now, until *M*A*S*H*.

Disappointed, Mom turned her pale grey-greens on me.

Oh, fuck, I thought, what am I supposed to say? In this nightmare *I'm holding hands with my parents for Christ's sake!*

"Um," I started.

"That's good," Mom said.

"Thanks," I replied.

"Let him say what he's got to say, Joanne," my father interjected.

"I am," snapped Mom, "Just let me do what I want." Then she giggled.

Shutting my eyes, I jumped in, "I just feel—"

"Yes?"

"Um, like...well, I'm a bit nervous about school."

"Yes," she agreed. "It's *hard.*"

"Yeah, and I want to just, well, um...*M*A*S*H* is starting in a couple of minutes and so, you know...." I trailed off, feeling mean. But they liked it.

"Then we should go quickly," my mother said, chuckling. "Wouldn't want you to miss *M*A*S*H*."

"I guess it's your turn," Dad said.

She smiled.

"Well," she said, preparing. "When I was *breathing* I had

63

a vision. I sensed a long tunnel with a bright light at the very end. I walked through to the light and what I saw was another life. A *past* life. One of *our* past lives."

She squeezed both our hands, to connect us, I guess. "We were all there," she said. "And in this past life we were a family, like now. Except in this life, Jason," she said, looking at me, her face tired and strained. "You and I were the lovers. The parents. And Paul," she looked to Dad blurry with softness and need, "*You were our child.*"

Dad froze. His fingers dug excruciatingly into my palm. On the Atkins' back porch, their youngest daughter, Melissa, fifteen, anorexic and (I thought) oh-so-sexy, shrieked, "Oh, my God, that is disgusting." *M*A*S*H* had started a minute-and-a-half ago.

"You are the child, Paul," Mom continued. "The child who needs help, nurturing. And in a past life, Jason and I, together we were able to give that to you. That gives me hope."

"I gotta go pee," I yelped, jumping up, throwing off their hands, sprinting down the hall and catapulting up the stairs three at a time. When I crept back through the hall an hour, two episodes of *M*A*S*H* and a joint-and-a-half later, Dad was out back cracking old garden stakes in half with his foot. Mom lay on the couch, crying softly, quietly enough so that the Atkins wouldn't hear.

Tonight it takes me an hour-and-a-half to get my son to sleep. Jillian insists that we not train him, that we lie with him until he sleeps, that he not be allowed to cry. So he's two-and-a-half years old and still needs us to lie with him, still wails and cries and howls. He thrashes back and forth, catches me three or four times in the face with his clenched fists. So many times, when Seth won't go down (that's the phrase we rental types use for putting our kids to sleep), I catch myself wishing he would *go down*, go down in such a

64

way as to never get up again.

When he finally surrenders I tiptoe stiffly to the garbage can and retrieve the torn pieces of Mom's lawyer-letter. Sticking them in an envelope, I grab another piece of paper and, sitting at the kitchen table, write across the top:

Dear Dad,
This is for you.
Jason.

What we don't tell our kids: when we hate them; when we despise every inch of their being; when we ache to rip into their flesh with our fingernails, to grab them by their chicken-wing shoulders and shake them until they crack, throw ourselves on top of them and scream into their little faces, *Close your eyes! Close your eyes! Close your eyes!*

If you were a kid, that would fuck you up.

The Thing I'm Most Afraid Of:
1. That this is what he'll think of me.

MARY SWAN

By the Sea, By the Sea

"Each physician should counsel those over whom he
has advisory charge of the dangers incident to a
prolonged exposure in the ocean"—*British Medical
Journal*, 1904.

"...and on Tuesday I called on the poor McIntyres,
whose daughter Mary died of overbathing last summer
in Ostend"—W. Lumsden, *Rambles Through the Shires*,
1906.

You have probably seen photographs of Mary McIntyre, you
may even have one on the wall in your den, in a box under
the stairs. Sometimes she stands at the back, one hand resting on someone's shoulder, or sometimes she sits beside
others on a settee, staring straight ahead. She's the one you
can't imagine smiling, although in fact she had a lovely
smile.

Her clothes are unremarkable. You can't see the colours,
of course, but they are usually shades of brown and beige,
often different shades in the same dress. Her mother has
always preferred brown and she chooses the fabric; it has
never really occurred to her that the tones she loves may not
be the best for Mary, whose hair is the colour of tea with
not enough milk. It looks darker in the photographs.
Drawn back smoothly, making her face look even rounder,
and her eyes appear dark too, although they were really a
flat bluish-grey.

Unless you looked very closely you probably would not
notice that her left shoulder is a little higher than the right,
the result of a slightly twisted spine, perhaps an accident of
birth. Half an inch higher, say, which does not sound like
much, which does not even look like much when you bring

out the old wooden ruler from your desk drawer. But it was a lot for Mary McIntyre; it may explain everything about Mary McIntyre. Or it may explain nothing at all, it may be incidental and have nothing to do with the things that happened. But someone should understand, or try to. Someone should know about Mary McIntyre and how she looked in that long dress. Someone should know about that summer in Ostend, and the way she vanished from the pictures.

The crossing was rough and her mother's head ached and there was trouble with the luggage and her father had to make a scene, even though he hated to, because it was so often the only way. Afterward he went out walking to calm himself and her mother rested and Mary McIntyre sat in a chair by her open window, listening to the soft *shush* of the sea and trying to make out its oily black surface by the light of the stars. And perhaps she thought about a new place, a new start, or perhaps that never occurred to her. She was a dreamer, something you wouldn't have guessed from her rather heavy, round face, her flat eyes, and often in her dreams she sat just so in a sunny garden, or walked a sandy path, carrying her bonnet by the strings in one hand. In the house where she grew up every sneeze made her mother flinch, every bump or scrape would have her in bed with blankets and potions, a cool hand on her forehead testing for fever. Perhaps she learned it early, this retreat into dreams. Or perhaps it was always her way.

Things might have been different if the others had lived. It was never easy for her mother; her father heard the screams, pacing downstairs or out in the street, and wondered what kind of brute would come to a woman again after that. He tried, he did try, but the tiny stones were planted in the churchyard one by one until Mary lived a year and then two and they began to believe that she was real. Not quite whole, perhaps, although they never would have said, even to each other. The slight curve in her spine that caused pain, from time to time, and the way she was— not simple, not that, but somehow removed. She could read and write and figure, she could learn anything if she put her mind to it, but she didn't often try and to keep her attention fixed on a piece of sewing, a little polite conversation, was next to impossible. At times she said the most peculiar things. A stranger would notice it, a number did that summer at Ostend, but her parents gave no sign.

So here they are at breakfast the next morning, Mother a little pale but otherwise recovered and Father rubbing his hands together before picking up his fork and Mary McIntyre saying that she will not, after all, go into the sea that day.

She doesn't know why she has said it. Her father raises his eyebrows and says, Very well, and she knows that he will talk about the weather a little, and perhaps remark that the dining-room is not so crowded at this hour. And then he will mention the cloudless sky again, and say that they have come here so that she can bathe and take the sea air, and then he will pause so that she can explain, but she won't be able to explain. Perhaps it is a premonition, or perhaps a dream she had once and in that dream she reached out a hand under water and someone turned to her very slowly; she saw the face and woke herself screaming. Although no-one came running, so perhaps the screaming stayed inside the dream.

She knows that they have come here for her, rather than to Margate or Lowestoft like other years, and she knows that it is only partly for the sea air. More to avoid those familiar faces who ask after her aunt and uncle, who cluck their tongues over poor Charlie and enquire after her own health, having heard something of her collapse. Perhaps her parents are also tired of being reminded but she does not really think of that, so bound is she by her strange, dreamy pain, so used to the way they take care of her. So certain that this rift in the family, the empty places at the holiday table, are all her fault.

Everyone thought it was the first time. The shrieks and loud voices in the attic, the closed door of her room. They didn't know—did they know that it had been going on for years? Charlie saying, Can we go and play? and her mother's face smiling at where they stood, her aunt too, saying, Run along now, off you go. The way she longed to step into their safe world, to take one step over the drawing-room threshold, and the way she knew it was impossible to do that. Their distant smiling faces in the steam from the silver pot and Charlie tugging at her hand, drawing her off to the garden, the shed, the attic.

This is what people do, Charlie said, although he had only the haziest of notions. Pictures in those books hidden behind the shelves in his father's study. Mary McIntyre's poor pale flesh was nothing like that, but she kept still like he told her and after a time he discovered that it was better if he hurt her a little. How did her mother not notice, rubbing different oils over her crooked back? Even in the flickering light she must have seen the bruises on arms and thighs, in the hollows of collarbones. Charlie saw them himself sometimes, and felt a little ashamed and more than a little amazed at his power. Once he gave her some sweets, flecked with lint from his pocket.

When they were discovered Mrs. McIntyre felt her hands go cold and she looked at her brother, his face transformed by rage and the flick in his eye when he caught hers and looked immediately away, so fast that only her icy hands told her she'd really seen it. She'd never told a soul about those times he held her down, the pain and his sweaty boy-smell, but in that flick of the eye she almost screamed at his

71

whiskered face, the cake crumbs on his vest, the pale napkin still clutched in one hand. Just for a moment and then she heard herself speaking calmly but no-one else seemed to, the bluster and the noise and Mary weeping, Charlie cuffed out of the house and down the street, her sister-in-law gasping into her handkerchief.

Things might have been different then. Marooned in her room Mary McIntyre slept and slept, yet still somehow felt she was waking. Until Charlie was sent to a new school where he took diphtheria and quickly died; then some horror knocked her from her feet and rolled her about without mercy. Months passed that are lost to her now although their story may be hidden in the lines around her mother's mouth, the dark bruises that will remain beneath her eyes for the rest of her life.

Someone should know about Mary McIntyre and how she felt that first morning after breakfast, for of course she did go to bathe; there was never really any question. Her parents waited on the shore, sitting straight in their little rented chairs, and someone should have heard her teeth chatter as she pulled on her costume, known the smell of wet wood and dried salt and the shock that went through her at the first touch of the cold hand of the sea, the cold licking tongues of the sea, welcoming her back.

She'd been to the seaside before, of course, and paddled for hours when she and Charlie were children. Every year their families holidayed in Folkestone, in Lowestoft or Margate. By the time she was old enough to look forward to things they were getting ready to change, but there were still a few years when Charlie looked after her well, tipping a bucket to make a sand tower, helping her to stand when she had fallen, although he was only half a head taller himself.

In those days it was always hot and clear and she remembers people sitting around a table and her father's moustache moving as he says that you couldn't get better weather anywhere, not even in the tropics. The men swam every morning and the children splashed at the water's edge and even her mother once took off her stockings and clenched her toes in the sand. The end of an afternoon, holding Charlie's sticky hand, grains of sand rubbing between their fingers. The sun still warm on the top of her head for she carries her bonnet by its strings and no-one tells her that she must put it on. Her father and uncle walk in front, their shirt sleeves rolled up, and her mother and aunt come behind, holding on to each other and laughing at something, perhaps the way their feet keep slipping. In a moment she and Charlie will say that their legs are tired and their fathers will bend down from their great height and swing them up through the air. But it is the moment just before this that she recognizes in some way. The hot sun, waves, the faint sound of a band playing somewhere and the tall, gentle shapes surrounding her; it is this moment that hovers at the edge of all her dreams.

So it cannot be the novelty of the sea that explains what happened that summer, and not the seaside either. A foreign one, it's true, but one large hotel is much like another, and the promenade, the pier. Differences perhaps in the sanitary arrangements, but even these are not so great. And the sound of French, of German and even Flemish, but as her mother remarked last time at Margate, with the babble of accents one might as well have been in a foreign country.

What was it then that made everything seem strange, and strangely charged? Perhaps she was changing, Mary McIntyre that is, perhaps she was on the verge of some great stepping out. Perhaps if death had not stepped in she would have clasped her life, and run with it. Or perhaps it was oily Death all the time, sidling closer, nudging her shoulders, her chest, twining round. Perhaps that was the thing that coloured it all.

Someone should know about Mary McIntyre, and yet it's so hard to keep her in focus. Her outline blurs, as it does in those photographs, as she herself faded out. The sound of her voice no more than a murmur against the tinkling of silver spoons on saucers, the competing bands from the park, the pier, from the great hall of the Kursaal. It becomes harder and harder to know her first thoughts as she comes awake in the mornings, to know her mind in the dining-room as she cuts carefully at her meat while the fair-haired waiters move soundlessly from table to table. The midday sun darts now and then through the high windows, sparking on cutlery already polished to gleaming, and it strikes the lines around her father's eyes, the cords in the thinning neck above his collar and she sees that he is growing old, that perhaps he will die soon and that even then things will not really change. She will trail behind her mother forever, from place to place, in and out of season, and the thought makes her incredibly weary, leaves her suddenly without the strength to lift her fork to her mouth.

Across the table her father works his tongue at a bit of gristle lodged in his back teeth; as far as he is concerned foreign meat is always suspect, although he keeps this conviction to himself. He is a decent, baffled man who fears he has mis-stepped somewhere. He suddenly thinks of bells and white clouds and his wife's hand on his arm and remembers that he felt ready to take on the world. Now the sunlight through the windows is uncomfortably warm; he watches his daughter dreaming, her fork halfway to her lips, and wonders how he could have forgotten to do that.

Mrs. McIntyre is also uneasy about the meat, but supposes that she will get used to it. She is a woman of hidden but strong opinions who should have had more to organize than a small household, rounds of visiting, occasional excursions in season. Who might have, in fact, if all those gravestones hadn't battered the life out of her, left her watching her living child, dreaming again, with a helpless mixture of love and despair. Mary's hair pulled back smoothly, covering her ears which fold out a little at the top, just like her father's, her face inclined to plumpness without the bloom of health and her awkward mouth, again so like her father's that her mother can't help thinking of all those small bodies, how one or two had thatches of her own dark hair, how things might have been different.

She stops those thoughts though, just as she stops the pang she feels at the sight of her own mottled hand, reaching out to take a roll from the basket. The rolls are fresh and slightly warm; everything here is as it should be and the waiters anticipate every need without intruding. This is the only way she knows to keep chaos at bay. Breakfast and a stroll, luncheon and a rest, perhaps a concert in the evening. Life can proceed in a strange hotel much as it does at home. She knows that only marriage will be the saving of her daughter and the sight of her own hand suggests that it is not too soon to think about that, to make the acquaintance of some of those mothers whose sons trail, reluctantly or attentively, through the reading-room, the picture gallery.

Looking at her husband, his cheek bulging as he works at his teeth, she counts her blessings. She would have done anything to get away from the home where she lived under the shadow of her brothers, and sometimes under their weight. And it was just luck, really, that her husband was still as he had seemed when she first met him—a kind, serious man who took care of things but rarely interfered. He would agree, she is sure, that it is time to think about Mary's future, to think about committing her to someone else's care. And perhaps, in one way of thinking, a European would be quite suitable. Less likely to remark the long silences, the occasional blurting out of the strangest things. And that business with Charlie—but she stops that thought as quickly as it flashes in her mind. She does, however, permit herself a brief dream of some years hence. A courtly son-in-law and the soft curls of grandchildren, the way they smell when she hugs them close.

As it turned out none of that happened and Mrs. McIntyre herself was dead within the year, so the dreary round of days that Mary foresaw would not have come to be either. Although it may have, if she herself hadn't stepped from the picture. The final shape determined by each piece slotting in in a particular way, a particular order.

What happened next will be recorded in a stack of dusty records somewhere, a chance combination of streams and currents that comes, once or twice a century, to the coast around Ostend. The air remained cool but the sea became warmer and warmer and seemed to deepen its colour, the blues and greens as intense as jewels. The breeze on the shore carried the faintest hint of spice, and a barely perceptible rattling, clacking sound. And while her parents sat up straight on the beach in their rented chairs, Mary McIntyre gave herself to the sea again and again. It rolled her around, it rolled around her, she paddled in the shallow warm water and even ducked right under, pulling herself clumsily at first with her arms, her struggling feet, but finally opening her eyes and seeing many things clearly.

Back on the shore where her parents wait it grows crowded and noisy, hawkers everywhere. Her father wishes he'd brought his pipe; he'd thought about it but assumed there would be too much wind, too much trouble fumbling with matches and tobacco. There is a wind, of course, but a mild one, just whispering over his cheek, barely ruffling the sleeve of his wife's dress. They have marked the position of their daughter's ochre-coloured machine and a good thing too, for after an hour the sea is dotted with them and several are a similar shade. He pulls out his watch and remarks that the driver is over time again, not knowing that the driver is quite content to tarry if someone slips him a half-franc along with the bathing-coupon. Mrs. McIntyre says that she supposes that a few extra minutes won't matter, and that the bathing seems to be doing a world of good, Mary's complexion clearer and her back hasn't ached for days. And meeting her husband's eyes she smiles and he does too, until a newspaper vendor taps him on the shoulder, offering yet another copy of *La Chronique.*

Someone should know about Mary McIntyre and what she thought or sensed, looking out on that vast expanse of scented sea. Looking out toward Margate as she had looked out from Margate, looking out on herself looking out and knowing that she was different. If she cupped her hands round her eyes and looked through she could have been the last person in the world, or the only one, and if she had thought about it she would have been surprised that this didn't frighten her. Quite the opposite, in fact.

When her extra time was up she left her costume in a heap, her stockings sticking a little as she pulled them on because she hadn't taken time to dry properly, so eager was she, in those first few days, to open the door and step out, to carry it all with her into the world.

The mothers had arranged for her to walk the Digue with Gaston in the afternoon, and so they strolled with other couples, with families and groups of girls and young men. Gaston stroked his spotty moustache and spoke of his delicate health, the many treatments taken, and he recited some verses he was quite proud of, but allowed that perhaps they suffered in English. It was very warm; perspiration beaded the sides of her nose, her upper lip, and Gaston ran a finger beneath his collar. Looking out at the rows of bathing-machines she remarked that they were just like people really, and he wrinkled his pale brow.

And as they walked on she felt impatience building until she could have screamed with it. To feel this unyielding surface beneath her feet. To be hearing about Gaston's frail constitution when she felt herself bursting with good health, with luck. She thought of those walks taken with her mother for as long as she could remember. The creak of the gate, the quiet prayers, the two tears that crept down her mother's cheeks. Sometimes it surprised her that there were only two, and sometimes that there were still two. But she had not joined those tiny mounds in the churchyard; she had survived and she felt that now as a triumph instead of a monstrous error.

Someone should know about Mary McIntyre and the way she closed her eyes for a moment, breathing in, hearing the sighing water, the far-off voices and the closer call of sea birds. Feeling the way her heart slowed down, her rough edges smoothed out.

That morning they had gone to the lace market in the Place d'Armes, her father slipping away immediately to the reading-room in search of an English newspaper. Her mother and Gaston's made slow progress through the market, stopping frequently to exclaim and rub things between their fingers. And Gaston remained stubbornly by her side, carrying a few packages and fumbling for his white hand-kerchief. Out of sight of the water she was dazed, she hardly heard a word he said. Straining for the sound of the waves, for the call of those wheeling birds. She began to realize that it had become an urgent thing, that some balance had shifted so slyly that she hadn't even noticed when it had happened. Harsh sunlight bounced back from the buildings lining the square and loud voices and laughter beat at her ears. She tried to call on whatever the sea had given her, that ease in her manner that made her mother smile and pat her hand, that sense of becoming that made each new day a welcome thing. But it had gone, it was gone, and she was left a jagged shell in a hard-edged world, not knowing if she would scream or weep.

So she says some words to Gaston, she doesn't even know what words, and turns and walks quickly away from the square, from the town, walking faster and faster until she hears only the rasping slide of her soft shoes. Gaston starts after her but she moves so quickly, he hasn't really heard what she said, perhaps she is ill, he looks back to where he last saw his mother, searches for her lavender hat, looks back to see the flick of Mary McIntyre's brown skirt as she disappears round a far corner, and coughs briskly into his white handkerchief, wondering what to do.

At luncheon she explained that she had suddenly felt ill, that the bathing had restored her and she was quite fine now, only a little tired. Later, her mother placed her silver brush on the dressing-table and said that she supposed that it was all right, and her father said that he thought Gaston a poor sort of fellow anyway. And they agreed that she was getting older, that perhaps they should let go a little, and they agreed that the bathing seemed to make her happy and that, after all, was what they had come here for. After that Mary McIntyre went down to the beach twice a day and sometimes more and the drivers began to watch out for her, and her extra half-franc. On the promenade her mother took her father's arm and he bent his head, in his courtly way, to hear something she had said.

The sea stayed warm and it was warmer on shore now and they all rested in the afternoon. Gaston and his mother returned to Liège where he would soon meet the pale woman who would become his first wife. He will bury her and two others, clutching his white handkerchief in a changing world, and as an old man he will come back to Ostend to consult another specialist, will sit in a waiting-room in a stray shaft of sunlight and wonder at his sudden unease, at the thought that things could have been different. Then someone will call his name and he will stop trying to remember whatever it is that he has forgotten.

And Mary McIntyre slept without resting, moaned and kicked in the underwater light of her room, the green shutters closed against the afternoon sun. Her appetite dwindled and a doctor, strolling past her on the terrace with his hands clasped behind his back, might have noticed, fleetingly, the light in her eyes, the colour in her face. The air was warm and one day, hurrying to dress for dinner, she opened her wardrobe and caught a glimpse of blue between the brown and beige sleeves and pulled out a shimmering dress like nothing she had ever seen. The way it fell about her, the ripples of colour like deep water splashed with sunlight; her hands trembled as she hooked it up.

In the dining-room she thanked her mother and talked on and on, her eyes sparkling and her cheeks flushed. Raising the fork to her lips and putting it down, untasted. And across the table Mrs. McIntyre felt a cold hand at her heart and knew that this was what she had been waiting for.

If someone had seen Mary McIntyre in that blue dress things might still have been different. If someone had held out a human hand, even then, she might have known at once the truth about the soft fingers of the sea. But no-one did. The dining-room was full, people talked and laughed quietly over the faint sound of the waves outside the dark windows. The fair-haired waiters stepped softly between the tables, their thoughts far away in their own country.

Each piece fit where it did, creating the perfect space for the one that came after, and the one after that. And some time during the night the sly currents shifted, rolled back to slide onto white sand shores, beneath chattering palms. By morning she was delirious with fever; they sent for Dr. Garnier, who shook his head, and then there was nothing left but the watching and waiting.

Someone should know about Mary McIntyre, but no-one ever will. She remains as remote, as mysterious as the person who sits next to you on the crowded bus, brushes past you on a busy street. Even someone who was right there could only guess at the things she dreams on the ochre-coloured steps, in her rumpled bed, the things she goes on dreaming. Dreaming the beach at Ostend, a cool wind brushing her cheeks, combing through her loosened hair. Dreaming the wild smell of the sea, the cries of spinning birds. Dreaming that her life will go on and on, that she will be there until the story ends.

On the Border

It was a hot day. He was killing chickens for all the old women and the knife was sticky and terrible. He threw each severed bird to the ground where it jerked and beat its wings, and when it was still a woman lifted it by one taut foot, holding it well away from her body. Dark splatters held down the dust, in places. The other women stood together, shaded by the brims of their floppy hats, talking about children and grandchildren. And noticed, suddenly, that he lay face down in the dust and the blood and the feathers, not moving. For a terrible moment it seemed that he had cut his own throat, by mistake.

And then everything else was moving, everyone running; they turned him over and a foreign girl tried to make him breathe. She plucked a curled white feather from his chin before she covered his mouth with her own. The women's voices twittered above her head and their splattered shadows bobbed and swooped at the edge of her vision. The tip of a long blond braid brushed his empty eyes. She saw that her hand had left a dusty streak across his face and she wanted to stop and wipe it off, but the nurse came and the ambulance, and they drove away in a great hurry although they knew there was no point. He was an old man, not given to troubling anyone; he died without a sound.

When they told his wife two women stood to catch her as she fainted, as they had expected she would. They were in the laundry-room; they eased her on to a pile of waiting sheets and dabbed her face with water from a sprinkler bottle. A large bladed fan circled slowly over their heads. They straightened her thick glasses and led her to her room, one on either side and several behind. It was very quiet. They passed a man and a young boy digging in a garden, spades whispering through the dry earth.

It was a hot day, but the room was dark and cool. When they opened the front door the first things they saw were his slippers, side by side, waiting to be stepped into, and they thought she might faint again, but she didn't. They stayed with her through the long afternoon, speaking of all their losses, husbands and sons. Her neighbour, coming home, slipped through the net of hidden voices, feeling the handle of the door suddenly cool and smooth in his hand. His wife brushed out her long blond hair, and they lay down to sleep.

Later, the widow began to wail and cry out loud. Next door the girl woke and turned to her husband; he lay on his back, lips slightly parted, and she closed her eyes against his sleeping mouth. On the other side of the wall someone told Leah to take a pill, and there was quiet.

The daughters arrived with the last bus from Jerusalem, late in the night. They spoke softly, made coffee and tea. One dropped a spoon and giggled like a child at the sudden sound. They walked about in their hard-soled shoes for hours and their footsteps echoed, as in an empty house.

All the next day the widows came and went, carrying plates of biscuits and cakes, different soups. They walked her in front of the house, one cupping an elbow on either side. She was smaller than any of them.

In the late afternoon they carried Yoav down the winding road to the cemetery, near the river. Some of the men had just come from the fields and red dust coated their shoes, legs. Leah moved like a sleepwalker between her two tall daughters. Her eyes, behind the thick lenses, were very pale, and her feet barely marked the ground. The place was ringed with eucalyptus trees, grown tall, and long wild grasses, bamboo. To the east, the dusty hills of a hostile country. His friends made short speeches as the shadows crept in. They put Leah in a car with her daughters, and it was finished.

It was hot. August, the killing time. The floors of the rooms were tiled, smooth, and all the shutters were kept closed. Primitive air conditioners hummed and the rooms were dim and almost cool. So hard to open a door and step outside, in August. To step into light so bright; even the flowers, violent reds and yellows, attacked the eyes. To open a door and step outside, feel the heat wrapping around the body, sweat forming in the places between fingers, in every tiny crease. Every day the sun stabbing down from a hard blue sky; it had been so for months, every day as bad as the day before. Late in the afternoons a teasing breeze rattled the branches of palm trees, a warm breeze that died almost as it began. And always the night fell down, thick and still; nothing moved. People fought with their friends and punished their children, fell from ladders and tangled their hands in machinery. People stretched tighter and tighter, in August.

Leah came back from visiting with her daughters and said that someone had been in her room. She stood in her neighbours' kitchen, kneading her fingers, one by one.

"You didn't hear anything?" she said. "You didn't see anything? Ask Allon when he comes home, maybe he knows."

"It's very odd," Allon's wife said, later. "The key was with her, someone must have an extra key. The lock wasn't forced, I looked."

"Did they take anything?" Allon said, unbuttoning his shirt, running his hands through his dusty hair.

"That's also strange," she said, "they took strange things. An umbrella. Some old records. A wooden spoon. And she said that Yoav's clothes were all messed up, but she didn't think that anything was missing."

"Tell her to speak to Ezra," Allon said. "Tell her to get him to change the lock."

"I already did," his wife said.

"Then that should be the end of it."

Later, when the long shadows stretched across the grass, he walked with Leah through the garden at the side of her room.

"Yoav took care of it," she said. "I don't know anything about it."

So Allon walked with her through the garden and named each plant. He told her when to water, and exactly how much, although she didn't seem to be listening.

"It's a very nice garden," he said. "Yoav made it very nice."

But she didn't seem to be listening.

The carpenter came home late and angry, slamming doors.

"Wasting my time," he said. "I can't take a step without some old woman wanting something."

He drank from a bottle of cold water and rammed it back into the refrigerator; it rattled icily beneath his words.

"Nothing wrong with the lock," he said, "I've got better things to do. Why would anyone want anything from her anyway?"

His wife studied psychology, from educational television. She said, "It's natural, she'd just lost Yoav, her security. It's symbolic, you see, having the locks changed."

The carpenter snorted and went to have a cold shower. The water was tepid and he cursed in several languages. His wife looked through the kitchen window and saw herself walking away, with a white flower in her hair and a suitcase in her hand.

The night fell down, heavy and still. Allon's mother, moving through it, passed a lighted window. A young girl crossed a room, holding her heavy hair on top of her head with both hands. Her steps were violent, three strides across the room. Allon's mother walked faster; she was late for a meeting. But a caged girl paced through her mind.

The meeting-room was thick with cigarette smoke and everyone was tired, and tired of trying to solve everyone else's problems. Typewritten requests stuck to their hands.

"We should talk about what to do with Leah," Allon's mother said.

"It's very sad," the younger women said. "It's always very sad. But she'll get over it, with time."

Their heads ached and their children were all crying somewhere and their husbands would all be in bed asleep when they got home. Allon's mother said, "I've known her more than 30 years and she's never been able to get over anything, not without help. I remember when she came here...."

The younger women sighed and lit more cigarettes. They knew the story, as they knew all the strange sad stories of the past. Grandparents disappearing beyond the range of the high arc lights, orders shouted in a harsh language. Parents jumping from moving trains, hiding in cellars, fighting over mouldy crusts of bread. Leah appearing from the dark hole of Europe, a strange little thing, skittering along the dusty track like a frightened deer. She was somehow not all right, and they wanted to send her away. But Yoav, who never asked for anything, begged them to let her stay, swore that all he wanted in this life was to take care of her. The younger women knew the story, as they knew all those stories of the beginning. Sharing clothes and singing all night, fighting malaria and hacking in the dusty earth for hours. Years. They had heard it all before and they were tired; their heads ached and their eyes scratched and their children were all crying somewhere.

"Why don't we arrange for some course," the carpenter's wife said. "Something creative, something—"

"Let's discuss it next time," someone said. "It's very late."

"Next time," Allon's mother said.

Walking home she thought of her second husband. Killed by a sniper's bullet, down by the border. The day they were married the sky filled with strangely shaped clouds and they tried to read their future. They bought a sack of peanuts to share with the others, and began to eat them, walking down the dusty road from town. Strange, but after 30 years the sound of her footsteps is the splintering of their shells. She can feel a dusky powder on her fingertips, almost taste them on her tongue.

Leah washed the front step, over and over. She thought she saw footprints, creeping to her front door, and no matter how many times she scrubbed and washed, they were there to lead her in.

Allon's blond wife peeled onions in the main kitchen. She sat on a low wooden chair; all around her giant steam pots hissed and women shouted and banged heavy metal dishes. She recited a poem in her own language; something from school, a long time before. A pine bough, caressed by falling snowflakes. Tears slipped from her eyes. The onions, she said. Later she fainted and the women stroked her hot face and sent her home. Onion tears pressed at her eyes the whole way and she almost ran when she saw the front door. She splashed her face with cold water, holding it with her cupped hands. Kjerstin, she said. My name is Kjerstin and I come from a place where it snows, in winter, and you can read your words in the clear air.

"Kjerstin," a voice said, "Kjerstin, are you there?"

It took her some moments to realize that the voice came from outside, that Leah was scrabbling at the door, wanting in.

87

"Look," Leah said, standing in the open doorway, reaching into the pocket of her faded dress. "Look, he's still getting in."

She held out a silver pen in a hard plastic case. Fiery needles danced, straight to Kjerstin's eyes.

"It's not the same pen," Leah said. "Yoav gave it to me, for a present. My name was engraved on it. Someone took it, and put another in its place."

"What kind of person would do that," Leah said, turning away, letting the door close slowly.

"I think there's something wrong," Kjerstin said. "I think there's something very wrong."

She set a tray on a low table and sat down, her knee touching her husband's. "No-one would do that, why would anyone do that? And last week she said that one of Yoav's undershirts was missing. She's not all right."

"Of course she's not," Allon said. "Her husband's suddenly dead and she's all alone."

"What would you do," Allon said, dropping a match into an ashtray just before it burned his fingers. "What would you do if I went off to the army and didn't come back?"

"I wouldn't spend all day counting your undershirts," she said, and he smiled and spooned too much sugar into his coffee cup.

Allon drove through the fields all day in a rattling jeep. Checking irrigation lines, opening and closing valves, soaked by the foul-smelling river water and steaming dry in the August sun, over and over again. Almost every day he drove past the place where a bullet found his father, and he wondered why on this day he had stopped to think of it.

The border patrol found footprints near the fence, as the sun was going down. The men picked up their guns and went off to guard the perimeter, the children's houses; it happened, from time to time. The static from their radios

88

carried a long way, and orange flares lit the sky.

The carpenter's wife packed a small suitcase and hid it under the bed. She went out into the crackling night to look at her youngest son, who dreamed terrible things. Looking down at his sleeping face she thought that she might weaken, after all, and take him with her.

Allon's mother was translating an article for the newspaper. She spoke five languages easily; before Independence she had walked through dangerous countries in various disguises, setting up escape routes. As a girl of fifteen she had moved through an occupied city, carrying guns in her hollowed out school books. Now she lifted her hands from the typewriter and rubbed at her tired eyes, knowing that the shutters were closed. She heard the coloured flares rising, and remembered a night in '48. Remembered sitting alone in a dark room, listening to the pounding of the long guns and letting herself think, for a moment, that they could never survive.

Something scratched at Kjerstin's door, very late.

"Don't be afraid, it's Leah, it's only me."

She was wrapped in a cotton robe, her hair tumbled, her eyes small and vulnerable without her glasses; Kjerstin couldn't bear to look at her. The same cringing feeling that came when she saw Leah's faded underwear hanging on a line by the front door.

"Everything's dark," Leah said. "I plugged in the kettle and everything went out, what should I do?"

"It's probably just a fuse," Kjerstin said, slipping an old letter between the pages of a book. "Do you have extra fuses?"

"What do they look like," Leah said. "I don't know, Yoav fixed everything, I don't know what to do. Can you go to find someone?"

"Let me try," Kjerstin said.

Next door in Leah's room it was already stuffy, and very hot. A tall candle burned in the kitchen, the only light. Kjerstin climbed on a chair and began trying fuses. Leah's wild-haired shadow danced on the wall. With the sound of each flare rising she jumped and twitched.

"I hate the noise," she said, "I hate that noise. Like the war, like all the wars, with the big guns pounding at night. Yoav is gone and no-one can help me now, he'll find me now."

The fuse connected and the room jumped out at them, but Leah didn't seem to notice. She was staring down at her hands, rubbing her palms together, hard. "It was an accident," she said. "We didn't intend...he was a little man with broken teeth. We ambushed his truck. We only wanted the petrol, we didn't know what to do with him. We had no place for prisoners, no food for prisoners. He sat on the floor with his hands tied behind his back, crying and shaking, and I said I would shoot him."

The only sound was the rubbing of her wrinkled hands.

"It's all right," Kjerstin said softly. "I've fixed it Leah, and the noise has stopped and it's not dark anymore."

"Why can't he leave me alone," Leah said, as she closed the door. As the lock clicked.

When she first came to this place, Kjerstin saw everything. A man wheeling a baby carriage, with a machine gun balanced on top. Concrete bunkers, grown over with flowers and children's paintings. Now when Allon put on his green uniform and disappeared for a few days, a few weeks, she thought only that she would miss him, while he was gone. Nights like this when the sky was bright and anything could happen, she picked up a book and waited to hear that it was over.

It was a hot day and the carpenter came into the dining-room angry. He sat down at a table with some friends and said, "That's it. It's too much. It's craziness, that's all it is."

His friends said, "What do you care? Put in a few locks and keep the old woman quiet, what's the problem?"

An old man stood up, pushed in his chair. He was remembering a stormy meeting, near the beginning. Fists crashing on the table, making the coffee cups chatter. And Yoav standing up and saying, in his quiet way, that the day there was a lock anywhere on the kibbutz would be the day he would leave.

"Things change," the old man said, but no-one heard.

The carpenter finished his dinner, smoked a cigarette and felt better. He crossed the cool dining-room to tell Leah that he would put small hooks inside all the windows. But he wouldn't change the lock again. It was new, and expensive, and he had other things to do.

Allon's wife wrapped her blonde braids about her head and they walked through bright flowers to his mother's room. It was Friday and the place was noisy with children and grandchildren, eating and drinking.

"When did she tell you this?" Allon's mother said.

"The night they shot the terrorists."

"Ah," Allon's mother said, as if everything was explained. "Is it true?"

"I don't know," Allon's mother said. "We had prisoners here once or twice, in '48. By accident really. We never killed them, we sent them on as soon as we could, that's all. But Leah was some time on another place, it may have happened there. I doubt it, but who knows. We were all on one border or another, all those years. Things happen, in a war."

"But she is really frightened," Kjerstin said. "She thinks that he's come back for her, she thinks that now that Yoav's gone he's come back for her."

"Nonsense," Allon's mother said. "She's always been

91

afraid of something. Afraid that her children would hurt themselves, playing games. Afraid that there wasn't enough flour and we would all be hungry again. I've discussed it with the Health Committee; there's really nothing we can do. And she's still working, she still comes to the dining-room, actually she's managing better than I thought she would."

"But she's not," Kjerstin said.

"Ezra's wife thinks she should take up macramé and find herself," Allon's mother said.

"Ezra's wife watches too much television," someone said, and they laughed.

Allon's mother served coffee in glass cups and opened the windows.

"We're all being spoiled," she said. "There's nothing so terrible about a little night air, nothing wrong with being a little uncomfortable. We lived for years without even dreaming of air-conditioning. We survived."

The August heat oozed into the room. Allon lay on the floor with his two small nephews. They rolled a sponge ball back and forth; tiny bells were sewn inside, a clear, clean sound.

On a hot day Leah climbed three stone steps to ask the security officer for a gun. A small pistol, something. The security officer was washing his hands outside the dining-room. He had been up most of the night. His wife was sleeping with his neighbour and his oldest son wore a diamond earring and all he wanted was to be sitting down in a cool room somewhere. He raised his voice and shook water from his hands and Leah ran like a frightened deer.

When the carpenter's wife heard the story that evening she nodded her head and began to talk about phallic symbolism, but she heard her own voice, suddenly, and stopped.

"Someone should call her daughters," she said. "Maybe

she needs to get away for a while, maybe she just needs a change."

"Tell it to the Health Committee," Ezra said. "I'm tired."

His wife turned out the light, and thought that the summer would never end.

September was a slow, drawn-out sigh. A few white clouds appeared, small but promising. People sat out in the evenings, sipping iced drinks; quiet voices like the rustling of leaves on the trees. The carpenter's wife unpacked her suitcase and Allon's mother began to knit a small white blanket. Leah's old underwear danced on the line, making Allon's wife laugh out loud, although she was by herself. People began to recognize each other and waited for the rain, and the afternoon breeze was a slow, drawn-out sigh.

The prisoner came some time during a cool night. In the morning one of the widows called, Leah, wake up, it's late. Knocking on the front door. Later she said, I knew, before I even looked inside; it was the sound of an empty house.

It was six o'clock and the grass was still damp; her sandals left faint marks on the tiled floor. The room was murky, only the pale light that slipped through the open window.

Leah sat in a chair in a pale circle of light by the open window. Into the silence came the sound of her quiet breathing. Her glasses lay on the floor beside the chair, and her empty eyes were terrible. They took her away in an ambulance, and no-one was particularly surprised.

Max–1970

Max's father is teaching him how to fix the dishwasher. It is not going well. Saturday afternoon, a pale dead sky through the kitchen window, through the bare branches of the lilac tree. Something like opera on the radio. Max thinks that any minute now he will have to scream.

It's not like there's anything really wrong with the dishwasher. A low hum at the end of the rinse cycle, a few streaks on the plates and glasses. Surely not enough to merit this savagery, the way it has been disembowelled on the off-white linoleum, wires hanging loose. An open toolbox full of things that have names he can't even guess at.

In the living-room his mother is fitting his sisters' costumes and he can hear them twittering, the occasional squeal when a pin scrapes the skin. He pictures their pigtails flicking against their shoulders. It's Hallowe'en and they're going out as angels—what a joke. Max is tapping his foot on the floor, the frayed bell of his jeans almost covering his running-shoe. Three inches away from his father's nose where he's peering at something under the machine and Max knows the tapping will be driving him crazy but he can't stop. He sees the way his father's hair is growing back in strange, tufty patches, nothing like it used to be, and he looks out the window instead. Then up to the clock above it. He was on his way out to the plaza when his father appeared with the toolbox. Typical, the way they're always going on at him about making new friends and then telling him there's some stupid job to be done. With his father home from the hospital he doesn't have to look after his sisters so much, but they just don't understand how things work here.

"Why don't you invite them over to listen to some records," his mother says in that new cheerful voice she has.

By now they'll all be gathered behind Woolworth's, rolling cigarettes and striking matches on the pale brick. No-one will notice that he's not there, and even if they did they wouldn't wonder about it. They'll move on somewhere without him and at the moment this seems incredibly tragic.

"Well look at this," his father says suddenly and Max squats down, peering at a mess of wires and trying to see what's caused all the excitement.

"Do you see," his father says, and Max says, "Yeah, sure."

As he stands up there's a sudden jerk and a pain in his scalp that brings tears to his eyes, a chunk of his long hair snagged around a nut or a screw or whatever the damn thing is.

"Oh shit," he says before he can stop himself, but his father doesn't seem to notice, says, "What happened? Max —hold still, don't panic. I'll get the scissors."

"No scissors!" Max shrieks, and as he does there's a sudden memory of a chair in the middle of the kitchen in their old house, the tea kettles on the yellowed wallpaper, his feet swinging off the floor, the buzz of his father's electric clippers.

"Hold still," his father says, as if he had a choice, and now all Max can see is his father's fingers, gently unwinding. He can't remember ever looking at his father's hands, but he's sure they weren't like this. So pale they're almost greenish, shaking a little. Punctures and bruises on the back from his last hospital stay and Max thinks suddenly that it must hurt. Then he is free, rubbing at his scalp, a few blond strands wrapped tightly around an evil looking bolt.

"If you'd get a damned haircut that wouldn't happen," his father says, and Max thumps his feet as he leaves the room. He meets his mother in the hallway and she stops him by putting one hand on his shoulder; he can feel the

95

anger leaving him, as if she's drawing it out with that hand.

"There are just things you have to know Max," his father says, back in the kitchen.

"I already know how to use the Yellow Pages," Max says, but then he throws up his hands and says, "Just kidding," and his father lets it go.

Neither one of them has the patience for this, and Max wonders why he's the only one who seems to know it.

While Max puts the tools away his father hooks the dishwasher hose onto the tap. He can hear his sisters bouncing a ball against the wall of the house as his father turns the dial. The low hum is gone, but in its place there's a loud metallic rattle. He looks up sideways from his crouch and sees his father's still back, his right hand reaching slowly to turn the dial again, turn off the tap. He walks from the room, and Max hears the back door close quietly. With a sigh he wheels the dishwasher to the middle of the floor and unscrews the back again, then realizes he has no idea what to do next. Looking through the back door he sees his father sitting on the cold lawn, his knees drawn up to his chest, one hand pulling up little chunks of grass and letting them fall slowly from his grasp. After what seems like a long time Max's sisters appear, running. They throw themselves on their father, wrapping their arms around his neck. Then they all stand up and Max moves away before they turn around.

In the shower he tries a couple of numbers, using the soap as a microphone, but his heart doesn't seem to be in it. He plops the white washcloth on top of his head and folds his lips over his teeth, checking in the hazy shower mirror; his eyes startle him. Then he notices something red and bulging right in the middle of his chin and he peers more closely.

"Oh shit," he says and hears his sisters gasp outside, the sound of running feet. "Spies," he shouts, opening the door and releasing a swirl of steam. "I'm surrounded by spies!"

It's late when Max arrives at the party and he wanders from room to room, the music pulsing through him. He's covered his face with white makeup, almost sure that the spot on his chin is invisible. Hair slicked back, lipstick blood dripping around his mouth.

"You look sweet," a girl named Judy says, dancing by.

"I'm *Dracula* for Chrissake," he says, but she's already gone.

He keeps walking around until he finds the back door and lets himself out, keeps moving. He walks around the Crescents and the Roads and the Drives, under the cold stars. He misses his friend Rob and the way they used to race their bikes, the way they knew every tree, every blade of grass in town. All the things they never had to say to each other. The letters they write once in a while aren't the same, aren't even worth doing really.

Once, when they were in fourth grade their teacher pulled the world map down over the blackboard and then showed them a book with maps the explorers had drawn hundreds of years ago. After they'd all laughed at the sizes and shapes she told them to think about how hard it would be to make a map if you didn't already know how the world looked, or if you couldn't look down from a great distance. In the weeks before the moving truck came, Max walked around his town with a mapmaker's eye, memorizing every mound, every secret path. The distance from his doorway to his bed, the exact pattern of the cracks on the ceiling.

Max walks around the side of their little house to the backyard and sits down at the picnic table he should have put away weeks ago. Smokes a cigarette and wonders if his mother will comment on the smell of his clothes. There's no way of knowing what she'll choose to get worked up about these days. As bad as his sisters during supper, thinking she heard someone at the door, stepping over the toolbox as she got up to peek around the corner and coming back, laughing at herself. Fussing about whether she'd bought enough candy.

"Next year I'll have a better idea," she said, "it's just all so different here, I don't know what to expect."

Something in her voice that Max had never heard before, when she was talking to him, something in the tone and the way she met his eyes, like they were on a level.

All around him there are sounds of the neighbourhood shutting down. A garage door closing, the rattle of a garbage-can lid. A low whistle and the chinking of a dog's collar. There are things he can't help thinking about. The way his mother's shoes fall by the front door when she pulls them off after work, and how some time later she sets them neatly side by side. The way his sisters with their floating hair really did look like angels. The way his father used to play catch with him long after supper, the way the ball loomed out of the dark in the split second before it smacked into his glove, and how even if they could do that again, it wouldn't be the same. He wants suddenly, desperately, to be any age but what he is, to be anyone else.

His fingers are numb and he flicks his butt over the low hedge, for the people with the Siamese cats to find. His own house is dark except for the neon haze that comes from the top of the stove, the orange light over the back door, glowing to guide him in. He tries to imagine that this moment is long in the past, tries to imagine where he will be, what he will be doing on a Saturday night in October in ten years, in twenty.

Of all the things he might have considered, he could never have guessed that it would be this. Feeling the thick, humid air of a foreign country as it oozes through an open window, bringing with it the sound of calling voices, of traffic that never stops. Standing on a shaky ladder while a long-haired woman steadies the base. Holding three coloured wires that dangle from a hole in the ceiling, trying frantically to remember something his father once said. Certain that if he gets it wrong the whole world will go up in a blaze of light.

JOHN LAVERY

You, Judith Kamada

I was, you see, a larcenist. I did not belong in university. I didn't go. I stayed in my apartment.

My father had paid my fees. I could hear him calling me. Calling me with my own voice. Judy! JUDy! Calling me a thief.

But I could not match the nervous palaver of the hippiettes with their hair like strands of tinted glass, thick and sweet with pot smoke. They did not go to their classes either, but they belonged.

The cream-coloured walls of my apartment were stained with the voices of previous occupants, their pleas, their pleasures. The hide-a-bed mattress was crusty with their mucosal secretions, the bathroom smelled of their humid hair. They were my antecedents, if not my ancestors. Their presence was welcome.

A Nigerian giantess from down the hall asked me to tutor her daughter whose skin was so dark I felt sure it would leave a mark when she touched me. To my disappointment, it did not. This job led to others. I was, as a university student, assumed to know everything and I always said yes. So that I was soon spending my mornings learning what I was supposed to teach in the afternoon.

There was a bookseller where I bought or traded piles of books. The owner took back my texts at almost full price. He was my reserve. He could always negotiate a transaction that resulted in his giving me money.

And then.

And then winter came, I suppose. The heat had to be paid before the tutor. Only the Nigerian girl kept coming, with her skin like potting soil mixed with butter, and she was far cleverer than I was or ever had been. My bookseller bought back all the books that his inverted sense of business permitted. The rest he took on consignment. That is, he put them in a box on a table staggering already under its load of such boxes.

I left a letter at the registrar's office by which I withdrew from the university, and after that, I rattled through the city streets, the sun a slice of raw potato floating in the steaming sky. I walked for days, my stomach churned with hunger, my sides split with cold, but my vital organs were insulated well enough by the brittle foam of my anonymity.

One morning the phone rang. It was my bookseller. He had a customer with him who was interested in one of my books, *The Poetics of Vehement Disorder*, an obscure piece of unreadability about which I remember only that the author was a Russian anarchist, Usakanov his name was, Alexei, and that the introduction contained an exhortation to all comrades of conscience to throw the book away after reading it, and to all comrades of courage to simply throw it away. The bookseller asked me how much I thought I wanted, seeing as it was a difficult book to obtain.

"I don't know," I said into the phone. "$3.49."

"Seventeen dollars?" he answered. I heard him repeat this figure to the customer.

"The gentleman is agreeable," said the bookseller. "He is going to wait for you here at the store."

The gentleman's name was Michael Leicester. He was talking to the bookseller when I arrived, and without interrupting his conversation or even paying much attention to me, he managed to give me the seventeen dollars and the impression that I was to wait for him.

"I own a small grocery store," he said when we were outside, "on Fairmont Street. If you need a job, you can work there. I can only pay minimum wage. A little more maybe."

I attempted unsuccessfully to speak.

"Oh," he said quickly, "you don't have to say yes right now. Or no. Just show up when and if you want to."

And so I began to work at the grocery store, making pyramids of oranges, mopping the floor, doing the cash. Every evening at six I locked the door and began to walk. There was nothing inventive or exploratory about my walking. I was like a clown walking in front of a screen onto which are projected drawings of crooked buildings, with this difference that the clown casts a shadow onto the screen. I walked until I was too tired to walk any more, climbed up to my apartment, ate some toast that I made on the stove with a bent hanger, and fell asleep.

Michael Leicester was never at the grocery store. I had not even seen him since the bookseller's, a fact which did not prevent, which no doubt encouraged, his constant presence beside me, suggesting I turn the tomato cans to all face the same way, sighing at the flat-faced mothers palpating every lettuce, observing sideways the light-eyed, dark-fingered children.

Counterfeiter, said I to myself. Bald-faced forger. To print his face on your play money, simply because he showed two bits' worth of interest in you, a mere modicum.

Still, the grocery store was the pin of my existence. I arrived earlier and earlier. The diameter of my trudgings shrank until I was rarely out of eyeshot of its baying, moonblack windows.

There was a storeroom behind the grocery. One night, quite late, as I leaned against the wall under the storeroom window, too tired to keep walking but not yet cold enough to go home, I heard voices talking with animation. And although I could not make out what the voices were saying, I knew that one of them was Michael Leicester's.

I listened for a long time, as I might have listened to a recording of a grass fire. I returned every night, and every night, or almost, the storeroom discussions crackled distantly under the window.

And then it was Michael himself bursting into the grocery one evening at six.

"Closing time," he said, all vinegar and vim. "Where would you like to go for dinner?"

He decided I would like to go somewhere where they served smoked meat. After the quarried beef had been brought, he asked me, amid much oversized chewing, a number of anodyne questions about myself. And then:

"So what have you found out so far?"

The pointed impetus of his tone brought the belligerence to my cheeks.

"What do you mean what have I found out?"

"I know you've been observing us. I would just like to know why."

"I have not been obSERving anybody."

"I am to suppose then that you stand in the cold and eavesdrop for fun."

"I don't...." My combativeness melted, realizing instantly as I did that Michael was a man who could never really know me, could never wear the colour-scheme of my nature.

"I wasn't eavesdropping," I said.

"You were just curious then."

"No I was not just-curious-then." And after a time, "I'll find another job."

"Do so."

And you, said I, and you, when you grope in the dark, is it for something other than the light switch? For something other than something to make the dark go away? We are all moths, we all spend our lives banging stupidly into street-lamps while the whole, gentle, welcoming darkness waits. And if the storeroom discussions are my glim, what of it? And even if I say storeroom discussions when what I mean is your voice, and even if I say glim when what I mean is ...it reassures me, there I've said it, plain and simple, your voice reassures me, what of that? What is there in that that gives you the right to observe *me*?

"Unless," he said into my fulminating silence, "you would like to join us."

He pulled out his, formerly my, copy of *The Poetics*, opened it, read selected excerpts of the type: "The temptations of God have always done more to undermine man's moral nature than the temptations of Satan," and: "The greatest danger for the revolutionary is to seek peace, not with his assailants, but with himself," and so on.

"Those are all passages you underlined," he said. "Why?"

Satan, thought I, Old Gooseberry. And did well to do so, seeing as you are now reading them to me.

"I was researching a paper," I said, "on grandiloquent Russian sophistry."

He looked at me hard for a moment through the plexiglas panel that shot up between us, and then gathered his coat to leave.

"I could...," I said, observing the salty french-fry bits left on his plate, "I would like to join you."

And so began my brief time, if not on the outskirts, certainly not among the inner crinolines either, of Marxism-Leninism as a revolutionary's apprentice. There were two others with Michael, one named Dan, I forget the other one's name. Dan I remember because of his half-finger gloves and choker scarves. And because, so he said, he had sat at Marx's desk in the British Museum.

I continued in the grocery store during the day, and after hours I did whatever I could to be useful. There being no shortage of things to do.

Pamphlets. I mimeographed them endlessly and passed them out at subway entrances, feeling each one slip from my hand as today earth slips from my hand to cover a tulip bulb. And when the police told me to move along, I astonished myself by berating them with all the brassy recalcitrance of the unconvinced. Which did not please Michael. "Just disappear," he would say. "Did they follow you?"

Follow me. Me. For whom what was behind was a void. Something I never considered, that slipped around in back of me whenever I myself turned around. To think of this void as peopled with following eyes offended me, thrilled me.

There was always a picket line or a student demonstration somewhere to be driven to in Michael's Volvo stationwagon. I was often not sure who to root for at these events, student activists being usually, though not always, more despised even than capitalists. In any case, my principal function was that of deposit box for all the bits of paper with names and addresses that Michael gathered.

Above all, I organized courses, two at least every week, that took place in elementary schoolrooms with poster paintings and miniature desks, the school authorities, thanks to me, under the impression the course was about life insurance, the lecturer one of Michael's innumerable American friends flown up from New York or Detroit to expound historical materialism, say, or dialectics and the arts to the five sullen drill press operators with doughnut sugar on their lips that I had managed to talk into showing up during interminable phone conversations.

Much of all this was done in the storeroom, at my vegetable-crate desk. Too often against the background of the grass fire discussions, which were not as soothing listened to from close range. Intense, argumentative and mirthless, they revolved around the wording of a long document Michael was preparing, an ambitious plan for the progressive infiltration of the party. I did not have the theoretic equipment to follow all that was said, or shouted, but I understood well enough that the plan called for highly disruptive social action, too much so for Dan and the other.

As the weeks went by, Michael became more and more agitated, while Dan and the other were less and less often to be seen.

One night, very late, I was typing the manuscript that Michael desperately wanted to finish, and which he was afraid, desperately, to finish. He was very tired, although I was not. I never was, in his company. I extorted his energy, no doubt, and burned it up myself.

"You should get to bed," he said. "You're tired."

He set up a folding cot on which I lay down as instructed, and then he turned out all the lights except for the one at his desk and resumed working.

After a time he said, "I don't know if we're going to make it."

"Mmm?" said I.

"The word is the RCMP is out to nail us."

"Buy them," I said, like a pro, having seen Michael on more than one occasion give money to policemen. He laughed a noisy, humourless laugh.

"You can get out while the getting's good if you like," he said.

"I don't like."

"Well watch yourself then, Judith."

This comment, which contained his one and only ever nominal reference to me, and which today tightens my throat with a nostalgia that is surely a form of grief, did not, at the time, please me.

"Just get your paper written," I said. "I'll look after myself."

Again he laughed. Silently this time, but with humour.

Until the morning when I arrived to find the grocery store crouching under a fringe of giant icicles like meaty, glass parsnips, the windows covered with plywood sheets, the green paint peeling and black. I did not stop. The air had been sucked from my lungs through a hard tube in my throat, I expected every instant some plainclothes behemoose to block my way, to say my name from behind, "You, Judith Kamada!" I rode on buses for hours, terrified the police would be waiting for me at my apartment, my legs mewling as I crept up the stairs at last, craning my neck to catch sight of them before they me.

But they were not there.

No, I whimpered, childish in my bed, the grocery store matters enough to be burnt to a crisp, but I do not matter enough even to be questioned.

After that I stayed in my room, so saturated with loneliness I could not move. It stiffened all my joints, its narcotic fumes were in my nose and mouth, putting me to sleep for days on end.

It is when I am most separated from my life that I feel most alive. When my life is most like me, like a lifeless sweater I have been wearing for years, and hating, I have no desire to act or be acted on. And here I was wearing, hating, the absurd hope (me all over!) that I would hear footsteps in the corridor, that Michael Leicester would stop in front of my door, while my smug skin was cold all over with the opinion that I would never hear from him again.

Do not believe those who think they know what is happening to you. I and my skin were both wrong.

The footsteps came, the knock. My pulse soared, I could feel it in my palm as I opened the door.

"Judith Kamada?" she said.

Oh, I thought, a shiver passing through me, who *are* you? Her forehead was shiny with fever, her eyes were glazed. You are my twin. Not of who I am, but of who I would have liked to have been. You have stolen my one chance at being beautiful. She sat on my sofa, very self-contained, mute, almost prim.

"I'm not feeling very well," she said to explain her silence. And then, "I have a letter for you from Michael."

She handed me the letter. I stuffed it into my pocket where it squirmed and nipped like a trapped crayfish.

"Would you like some macaroni dinner?" I said.

She ate slowly, talking to me confidingly, restlessly, assuming I was a long-time communist, an error I did nothing to correct, mentioning many names I had never heard while I scrunched my forehead to appear concerned. Although I was concerned. So many people lying low, moving away.

I was seized, offended, by her viperine contempt for those die-easy party members who had scurried for shelter at some suburban cousin's.

"It is not possible to make revolution," she said, her ill eyes sparkling with disdain, "not here, not in this wingless country."

She curled up on the sofa, her back to me, and went to sleep.

The letter was addressed to "J. Kamada." In it Michael said that the person bearing the letter was quote an important human being unquote, and that, although I was under no obligation to do so and he would perfectly understand if I refused, he would consider it a personal service if I quote lent unquote her my passport. He looked forward to seeing me again once things quieted down.

I am still looking forward to seeing him again. I say that without sarcasm.

I always will.

She woke some time later, a gust of panic blowing over her face until she remembered where she was.

"Why are you looking at me?" she said.

Because you have stolen my one chance.

"Oh," I said, "I was picturing you in…in foreign capitals, Rangoon, Buenos Aires, Budapest, Paree. I think you should go to all of them at least once."

She took my hands then in hers which were burning and limp. I drew my hands away, and took hers in mine.

And we never mentioned Michael Leicester again.

Oh she was weepy and exhausted and got substantially

crankier before she got better, but she put the hep back into my step, the glide back into my stride, I had never had anyone to look after, I went out and bought real food, pored over chickens, palpated every lettuce, returned to find my apartment bulging with her bed-ridden odour, as if a kilo of frozen lichen had been put in the oven at 425° for seven or eight minutes. Is it possible, thought I, that I too smell so pungent in another's nose.

One day she got up and made some tea, drank half, hurled the cup across the room, threw open the fire-escape door and stepped out into the persistent rain that was shrivelling the snow and eating into the sidewalks. She stayed out long enough to become thoroughly wet, re-entered and said:

"You're going to do something for me."

She opened an exercise book full of names and addresses, and soon she had me running all over town, trick-or-treating, knocking on doors, meeting men in bars and beside shopping mall fountains, canvassing for money. There were those who claimed to have never heard of her, those who gave a few, and more than a few dollars, hoping no doubt it would buy their release from all further soliciting, and those who handed me thick, sealed envelopes.

She told me to take my passport to the offices of a certain smalltown newspaper. I got on a new bus that aspirated its way into the country where the fields were drying out in the crisscross spring winds. It dropped me off in a town made of bricks. I soon found the local paper.

"What are *you* doing here?" said an irritated voice the instant I entered. "As if I didn't know."

It was Dan, wearing shirt-sleeve garters and a visor. He took the passport and told me to come back in two days.

Which I did. He was quite drunk this time. He fanned himself with the passport that now contained her picture instead of mine, saying that Michael owned several other small grocery stores, that it was easy to be a communist when you were floating in equity, that maybe the RCMP arranged to have the Fairmont Street store incinerated and maybe Michael arranged it himself, that, in any case, the only reason he had taken an interest in *me* was because I resembled *her* and seemed pliable enough to get a passport out of. And so on.

"Yes," I said, "but you're not telling me anything I don't already know. Michael asked me about the passport long before I worked at the store."

I plucked the black booklet out of his hand and left, invigorated by the joy of lying.

A few days later, we bought her an airline ticket together.

And then she was standing in my doorway, shouting, "I'm leaving now!" at me, who was out on the sunny fire escape, unable to answer, unable to move. She walked back through the apartment, said, sharply, "Everything will go fine," and left. I waited and waited, but nothing happened, no sirens, no commotion, no crack snipers surrounding my building. No, no. Everything went fine.

Fine. Everything did go fine. I waited and waited. But she did not change her mind. She did not come back. I received a postcard of O'Hare airport. Unsigned. On the back she had written, "Thanks."

But I, had I made any attempt to convince her to stay? No. She was—what was she? She was inaccessible, superb, she knew how to move, to manoeuvre, she knew what to do with names and addresses, she could get people to get her money and passports.

She set me up. She stole my one chance. And I was glad she did. Having no more chances, I could just do the life gig, get married, work, miscarry, work, learn Windows, convince my husband to buy a Volvo station-wagon.

I walked around and around for years with a picture of her buried among the crumbs and grains of dirt in the bottom of my purse. For years.

While each day deposited its layer of forgetful sediment. I even managed to forget her name. Ca...? Carol? No. Karen? Perhaps. I don't remember.

Layer upon languid layer, with just a thin little green crust, where I plant my crocuses.

Ah but the earth has more faults than a human heart even. It shudders and cracks its toes while our wee overpasses buckle and we scream. Real beanstalks burst through backyards overnight and bring down giants that can breathe in blood.

Messages from Dayton appear on my screen:

judy, i post you verbatim this small terrifying piece from today's paper—police found the body of a woman yesterday in a cambridge park apartment. the landlord who was owed several months rent had requested police assistance after the woman failed repeatedly to answer her door. the cause of death is unclear although the woman was apparently suffering from severe malnutrition. found on the premises was a long-expired canadian passport in the name of judith kamada. thought it was you kid for half a half a second. any other j k's living up there? the piss right out of scared me it did nearly.

Look at me. Do you see me shake?

What has become of me? The life gig. The unhurried pursuit of a not too distant happiness. Is that not enough?

I cannot imagine what events could have led to such misery. I have not the intensity, the breadth of experience. She never got in touch with me. Never. I could not have known. I am not guilty of manslaughter. I am not. I am not. I am not.

The Breeze Being Needed

My father was, is, an ambulance driver in St. Catharines, Ontario, of Egyptian distraction, whose name was, *is*, Ossama Bashur (as is mine). He has been attempting for years to melt into the developed-occidental decor—12-handicap Lion's Clubber, campaign chairman for the vice-mayor—has been melting, therefore, like a red ice-cube into clear water. Because he *is* Egyptian, and was so even in 1947 when he arrived with his little post-war English tradesman's certificate and his stoutly Canadian wife (hi Mom). He has had, consequently, certain things happen to him—all part of the normal residue of human nature churning out its obtuse and self-congratulatory destiny—but certain things all the same, and as a result of these certain things, I was shipped off when I was three to the city of Madison to stay with my mother's elder brother and his Wisconsin wife where at least there was food.

I had a vision in Madison.

A sinewy woman was my Aunt J., with a wilted face, as if the pressure inside her head had dropped for an instant below atmospheric pressure, very strong and with acidulous breath, which led me to think she ate flowers. Moved by a sense of disciplined commiseration with her sister-in-law, she never let me forget that my true home was not Madison. "You're a Canadian, Ozzie," she would say to me. But I was still in a pre-geographic phase of life, my only nation was my bed, everything else a foreign territory where I might at any time and for no apparent reason be asked to report on the nature of my activities. I had at best the ghost of an idea what the word meant, the word "Canadian" that is, so that each time it was spoken it spread over my tingling brain like magic smoke, its billowy, white sound screening me from the fluttering dove of its true definition.

I say vision. A vision is generally held to be a hot and blasty affair associated with many fathoms of light. Not mine.

Although I did have one important clue as to what a Canadian, like I was, was. The clue was not contained in my memory, which was still something of a toy, an album of moments I played with only occasionally. Nor was it contained in the geo-political catechism to which my aunt regularly submitted me: "North America is a continent, Ozzie, divided into two countries, the United States of America and...Ca?...Can?...oh Ozzie! Kansas City's a city!" The clue was contained rather in the figure of a man of contradictory characteristics. He was tall and trim in his good clothes, gawky in shorts. His great-smile occupied so much of his face that it pushed his cheeks out of the way into his eyes which dropped out of sight completely. It was, to me, an analgesic smile that revealed, nevertheless, a mouthful of teeth so large and overlapping that they appeared to grind against each other painfully. He was my Uncle T., and the man to whom my Aunt J. referred when she said to me, "You're *just* like your uncle, Ozzie, he's a Canadian too, you know, your mother's brother, you haven't got any brothers, or nephews either for that matter, not yet, no."

No, my vision occurred in the chilly, semi-darkness of the second storey of Aunt J.'s duplex, as, weaving sleepily from my nation-room to the john, I passed in front of their imperfectly closed bedroom door. Aunt J. was not in my field of vision. Uncle T., on the other hand, was. From head to foot. Although it was not either to his head or to his foot that my attention was drawn, but, as was his own attention, to his sex. To its exotic pendulousness, yes. To its leonine hirsutitude, certainly. But above all to its colour. Uncle T. had a little bottle of paint in one hand, an artist's paintbrush in the other. And he was painting himself bright red.

A minim of my imagination was cauterized for ever and good. Even though the bedroom door was firmly closed when I returned from the john, and every time thereafter I attempted to confirm my initial observations, I could expect to review at any moment, willy nilly, the dark hairs running down out of Uncle T.'s navel and all but drowning his crimson, flamboyant mensware. I mused upon my vision at length, mentioning it to no-one. It excited me when I was excited, and calmed me when I was calm. It drew me relentlessly into my uncle's intimacy, its glowing secrecy surrounding me, pushing me toward him whenever we were in the same room. "What's got into you?" he would say, fending me off, and I, with my five-year-old, unmannered intuition, I knew that he was right to do so, that there was something false in my affection, something missing, it was not simply Uncle T. but both of us, me watching Uncle T., that was what I had really seen. I lay in my bed perspiring, seeing myself over and over in my own vision. Until finally it collapsed, the vision did, it turned liquid and drained into all the interstices of my understanding. I knew. I knew why it had been given to me, to *me*, to see Uncle T. Because we were Canadians. The only two for miles and miles. And a Canadian was a man, when he got to be a man, who painted himself red.

After that, I won all the 50-yard dashes and all the spelling bees, and only talked to Uncle T. to ask him to pass the macaroni please, sir. And when my Aunt J. said, "You're *just* like your uncle," I answered, because I so hoped she was right, "I am *not*."

I started Grade 3 in Madison, but I finished it in St. Catharines, the circumstances leading to my repatriation being as follows:

My father, having just returned from Quebec where he had gone with a group of local itinerants to pick apples, was in a tavern with the said itinerants when, encouraged by the accumulation of empty glasses on the table, he decided to tell a joke. He would never say what the joke was. As the punchline approached, he could not prevent himself from becoming excited, or his Egyptian-trained vocal apparatus from becoming clogged, with the result that he found himself giggling nervously at the joke he was not managing to put across, hoping to dislodge a little mirth from his confused listeners. His tense hilarity transforming itself into a drunken tantrum, he stomped out of the tavern, was struck by a car and, shortly thereafter, loaded into an ambulance where he regained consciousness in time to see the driver, a pink-faced individual with white eyelashes, slump dreamily over the steering-wheel. The driver's partner managed to bring the ambulance to a halt and immediately began massaging the driver's failing heart, while my father, essentially unhurt and instantly sober, jumped behind the wheel and lit out for the hospital all-sirens-ahead. No sooner had they got there than another call came in, another and another, so that when at last he stumbled homeward that morning he was drunk and giggling all over again, the driver having died in the night, and he, my father, having been hired without further ceremony to replace him.

Steady. Money.

This story my father has recounted any number of times, as recently as yesterday, but not, as I believe he should, to satirize the fruit-belt fraternity which instead of silently giving him a job to do, made him be a pledge and rushed him for years, eventually submitting him to an initiation rite worth a photograph and half a surprised page in the local newspaper, a rite whose donalduckleness distracted from its essential shame. No, he recounts the story because he is proud of it and because he likes to reaffirm his adolescent, pledgling admiration for the ambulance driver who gave his life that he, my father, might become a normalized citizen.

In any event, his first act in his new role was to recall definitively his banished son.

I shook my father's hand very dutifully, recognized my own wiry black hair in his, understood why my oddball name was the same as his name, felt his mysteriousness turning the air in my lungs to glass, all the while doing my utmost to silence the alarums drumming in my ears, to frap my cracking self, to stifle the name of Uncle T. swelling longingly in my throat.

Certainty is a stern quality, without nuance or play, domineering, desperate, appealing, strangely, to those who believe themselves least susceptible to desperateness and domination.

And I was as certain as the Sahara is certain: this man, my father, was not a man who painted himself red. Not a Canadian. I would not have it. He was a foreigner.

And here we are, half a lifetime later.

"I have a story for you, Ozzie II."

Stories, he calls them. Jokes they are, just jokes, millions of the unfunny things, kid's stuff and worse, all meticulously written out on file cards to be taken out during quiet stretches and run through, never to blow another one, the build-ups elaborated and adapted to perfectly suit his rolling butter-cream-eyed style and sing-song voice, the punchlines barely more than cues to his listeners to snort once shortly and ask for another, and I, during much of the same half-lifetime, bouncing from half-success to qualified failure, no sooner engaged as second sax in the 47th regiment sitting-down band than its funding evaporates and it turns into a bugle corpse, my pockets no emptier than the day I was born, my father out of exasperation putting me in charge of an eight-unit apartment I did not even know he owned, although he had 46 other units in various locations and part of a trailer park, and before I knew it I was Mr. Jacob P. Landlord making a chocolate mint housing two-thirds of the half-failures in town.

Of course my vision could not withstand the Canadian climate, the minim of my imagination remained cauterized but a minim is not very much, my certainty soon crumbled, I came to realize that if Uncle T. painted himself red that was his business, my exaggerated fondness for him broke apart into chunks of ribald hilarity, disintegrating further into chips of curiosity, still further into nothing at all, I forgot about the red paint, Uncle T. and Aunt J. too for that matter, not having seen them since even before they separated for lack of children. But if I let my vision sink into the sea with a hiss, I did not therefore grant my father—it being a further characteristic of certainty that the misapprehensions it nourishes continue to grow nicely even though the certainty itself rots away—did not grant him what everyone for miles around was more than happy to grant him despite his unbearable jokes, namely a full and unqualified, a model citizenship.

Toastmaster, realtor, high-sounding politico, ambulance driver, doer, dad. Although ambulance drivers too wind up in hospital beds.

"I grant you," says he, "I have devoted a great deal of energy into prolonging my life, which is only mildly embarrassing. Besides, now that I can consider my life distantly, inquisitively, without anger, without hope, as you might consider a thing, a fan say, spinning in its cage, a three-speed speeding fan, it makes a little breeze, good for it, it will do so for as long as a breeze is required and then it will not be a fan any more, so now that I can, now that each day begins with its puff of surprise, by chance, pure chance, Ozzie, we are not responsible for the breeze being needed, baa, if I put so much effort into being a good shit it is because nothing lasts like good shit, nobody throws it away because it's good, nobody eats it because it's shit, it just sits there and stinks less and less, embarrassing I grant you, but only mildly, I have a story for you, I got it from the orderly: Two men in a boat. Cigarette? says one. Sure, says the other. Got any matches? says the one. No, says the other. Me neither, says the one. So he fishes another cigarette out of the pack and throws it in the water. Know why?"

"Why," say I.

"So the boat would be a cigarette lighter. Don't laugh."

"I'm not going to laugh," say I.

"Where's the attlebaxe?" says he, the attlebaxe being my mother.

"She's coming," say I.

"Cultivate, Ozzie II, a sense of belonging, and they'll all stop noticing that you don't belong. Ingratiate yourself. Got another story for you, also from the orderly: Mister A: I bought a pair of pants today. Paid way too much. The salesman was from Cairo. Mister B: How do you know he was from Cairo? Mister A: 'e gypt me. Hardy-har. Me and the orderly on the same side at last. See what I mean? Only mildly. Ah, the attlebaxe."

In sashays then my stoutly Canadian, greying mother, high-heels and turquoise rings, necklaces like strings of beaming candies, her flowery dress drifting quietly over the wide plateau of her upper breastwork before falling over the edge and plummeting earthward, my mother, moved by an undemonstrative distrust in all who profess even mild competence in any field whatsoever, together with a cold-eyed, demanding sympathy for the unsuccessful, unlucky, undernourished, underdogged, underloved. In sashays the attlebaxe, delivers greetings: "How are you feeling? How are your movements?" and says, "Tobias and Jean are coming to see you."

Uncle T. and Aunt J., whom I have not seen since even

before they were divorced, reunited by Ozzie I's cancer. My heart leaps up.

"Baa," says my father, "Coming to see Ossama you mean."

"Now don't start," says my mother.

What, say I to myself, tension? In connection with Uncle T. and Aunt J.? News to me.

"Don't start what?" say I, lazily.

"Don't *you* start," says my mother.

"What?" say I.

Brief pause for silent, negotiatory calculation.

"Well...," says my mother, this being the usual prelude to her conclusive edicts, "your father would just rather not have had to send you to Tobias and Jean's, that's all. Men are proud. Perfectly understandable."

"If you want to know," says my father, unprepared to take the gag, "there was no living with you when you came back. Snarky little six-year-old smartass."

"Yes, well, there's living with him now," says my mother. "That's all that matters surely."

"So damn," says my father, "attached to them. Uncle T. this and Aunt J. that. Your mother found it very difficult."

"Well...," says my mother, "in the first place, you underestimate the thickness of my skin. I never minded cutting off the crusts just like Jean did. What *you* minded was of course just that, that I didn't. In the second place, in the second place, it was Tobias and Jean who got too attached to Ossama."

"Well...," says my father, this being the usual prelude to the collapse of his argumentation, "that *might* be true."

"Of course it's true. You gave them their best years, Ossama. You should know that. They did us a great service and they were very devoted to you. So much so, they decided not to have children of their own while you were staying with them. They thought it might be hard for you.

121

And then when you left, the children just didn't come. Terribly sad. Jean sent me letters and letters. It just rankled and festered, and finally they couldn't live with it. Jean was made to have children you know. Tobias too, Tobias too. Terribly sad."

The attlebaxe having chopped a small hole in my heart, I stifle the name of Uncle T. swelling longingly in my throat.

"Sometimes," says my mother, "I think the reason *we* were never given more children, and we certainly wanted them, was so that Tobias and Jean would not be hurt."

"Oh," says my father, "I thought it was the Mercurochrome."

"God," says my mother, smothering something in the crook of her throat, a guffaw perhaps, a sob, "weren't we stupid though."

"Mercurochrome?" say I.

"You don't need to know about the Mercurochrome, Ossama," says my mother.

"Baa," says my father. "Your Uncle Toby's highly scientific method for not having kids. Paint the appropriate areas with Mercurochrome before getting down to business. Supposed to kill the little tadpoles. Your mother had us doing it for a while. We used other things in conjunction. We weren't completely stupid."

The attlebaxe is trembling. She is laughing silently. She is never so silent as when she laughs.

I had a vision in Madison. A childish misinterpretation of adult ineptitude. Long forgotten in any case. Dropped into the sea with a hiss.

The ambulance driver consolidates his advantage:

"Besides, judging by the quality of the business we got down to, birth control was not the only reason your mother wanted us using the Mercurochrome."

The attlebaxe is shaking uncontrollably. It is the way she laughs. Her face is very red, her hair very white. One hand is stopping her mouth, the other is holding her necklaces so they will not rattle. Her eyes are deep in the eyes of the ambulance driver. He is grinning himself, like the White Nile, having flooded the attlebaxe's wide plateau with so much mirth. His prostate gland is blown with cancer. His eyes are deep in the eyes of the attlebaxe. They are both crying.

Tobias and Jean are coming, Uncle T. and Aunt J. having long since split up.

I am the foreigner after all. I have been supplied a passport, yes, but am refused the necessary visa to enter the country of this intimacy.

So I busy myself. Silently. At the edge of the breezeless sea. Pouring sand into the hole in my heart.

Naming Darkness

Daphne MacMillan, 21, Associate of the Royal Conservatory of Music of Toronto, opened her front door to the mother and daughter standing on her doorstep, their backs to the late, warm, September sun. The mother held her daughter closely by the elbow, and regarded Daphne with a steadiness that indicated a desire to look away.

The daughter stood perfectly still. She possessed an air of self-containment which, in a fourteen-year-old, gives an impression of brilliance. She was dressed in a simple blue seersucker dress and white oxfords, a little too perfect and young, her brown hair very shiny and parted at the side. The sunlight shone through the rim of one of her ears, making it glow.

A lovely girl certainly. But she did not possess the crackling, pale eyes of a lovely girl. She had no living eyes at all. Instead, two black wounded slits set her face into a crude and constant squint.

"This is Janice," said the mother. "Janice has been blind since the age of two—she'll be fourteen in December, won't she. Janice thinks she would like to learn to play the guitar."

The two sat opposite each other on cold folding chairs in the small music room that smelled heavily of carpet. The notes spun out of Janice's guitar like pieces of ice. She made a mistake, the notes turned into stones. She bit into her German spice cookie and began again.

They were not always German spice cookies. They were sometimes ginger creams, or peanut crisps, or chocolate crinkles, or snickerdoodles. Daphne made them.

She listened spellbound, Daphne did, to her new student who had already made such astonishing progress. The speed and clarity with which Janice executed her technical exercises inspired Daphne with a fear that entered her through her own fingers, a fear that was unquestionably a form of joy.

The doorbell rang.

"That'll be your mother," said Daphne, putting Janice's guitar into its case and the case into Janice's hand, licking a corner of her sleeve and wiping away the crumbs from around Janice's mouth.

"Is she making any progress?" asked Janice's mother.

"She's a monster," said Daphne.

"That, I hope, means she's doing well," said Janice's mother.

"Very," said Daphne.

The mother took her daughter by the elbow, looked at her with suspicion.

"Have you been eating something?" she asked.

"No!" said Janice.

Daphne had considerable difficulty in referring to the classical composers for the guitar by their actual names. Sor became "Sorehead," Carcassi "Carcass," Aguado "O-god-no."

Janice had little trouble playing the music of these fussy and dusty Latins once she had learned it.

But learning it was painfully laborious. She was obliged to memorize the music at the very outset. To memorize it physically, in her hands. Daphne taught her note by note, beat by beat, placing Janice's fingers on the fingerboard and indicating which strings to strike. Entire lessons were devoted to a very few bars, mere seconds of actual playing time. Music which had been learned one week had inevitably to be relearned in subsequent weeks.

Daphne could at least allow herself the luxury of letting her tears flow quietly, provided she did not sniffle, or let her voice waver.

Janice, for her part, when her frustration became severe, turned very white and spat viciously, after which she remained so still she seemed to tremble.

As a result, Daphne began calling her "Moby Dick."

Recital rehearsal. Janice performed the 18th Sorehead study perfectly. The other students, crammed into Daphne's living-room, applauded furiously. Particularly Chris.

The rehearsal over, and the living-room filled to bursting with rapid clouds of chatter, Chris looked for Janice, brushing the hair away from his forehead very intellectually with the heel of his hand.

"ChilDREN!" said Daphne. The clouds thinned. She regarded the unsettled sky of her silent students regarding her.

"Well that was rather painful. I remind you that the real recital is *next* Saturday, so you still have time to sign up for piano lessons somewhere. Or tuba or even youkaLAYlee lessons."

Puffy, altocumulus laughter.

"But now its time to *eat*. So if you'll direct your attention to the kitchen door, Moby has something to tell you."

Janice stood close to the doorframe, her excited smile and clumsy squint making her appear oafish and bright.

"Ladies and gentlemen," she said, "come to supper. Baked beans, and bread, and very good butter."

"*And*," said Daphne loudly into the cumulonimbus commotion of chairs, and standing up, and clapping, "Moby prepared everything herself."

"I know why you made beans," said Chris.
"Why," said Janice.
"They're the musical fruit."
"The musical fruit?"

126

"Beans, beans the musical fruit. The more you eat the more you toot."

"The more you toot?"

"Fart," whispered Chris into her ear.

Janice laughed outright and turned her face in the direction of Chris' voice.

He did not leave her after that. Not for two seconds. He was full of clever things to say. Such as: "God your tone is clear. You don't play a note, you etch it. I mean me, sometimes I think I've got like fur-bearing fingers."

And then the other students had gone home and it was time to clean up.

"Want a hand?" said Chris loosely.

"No no no no no no no," said Janice.

So Chris, ostensibly just watching, very silently moved the dishes so that Janice could find them more easily.

"Don't do that," she said very softly.

"What was that?" said Chris. "Did you break out into idle conversation?"

But she did not repeat herself.

And then Daphne, folding chairs under each arm, backed into the kitchen and leaned against the counter beside Janice to rest.

"Have you got any muscles at all, Chris?" she said.

But when he made a move to help her, she glanced at Janice and reconsidered.

"No no, forget it. They're not heavy really. Your beans were a big hit, Moby."

And then Janice stepped on Daphne's foot with such violence that Daphne cried out, letting go the chairs, which banged against her ankles. She clattered to the floor, sobbing.

"You know, Daphne," said Janice, adding water a tablespoon at a time to her pastry dough, "my darkness is not always the same. Sometimes it has a rhythm to it, sometimes it is very smooth, sometimes it makes a rustling sound like paper. And sometimes even it seems to be on the verge of disappearing. When I was young I used to give names to my darkness. My darknesses. I still do sometimes."

"Really," said Daphne, interested, but too occupied melting chocolate to notice that Janice had reddened. "What kind of names?"

"Oh I don't know."

"Well right now," said Daphne, observing her chocolate closely because it was getting very warm. "What kind of name would you give to your darkness?"

"Oh I don't know. Domesticity."

"Really," said Daphne, looking up. She knew that Janice wanted her to like the name, and she wished she had been listening more closely. Perhaps then she would not have been so puzzled by it. So disappointed.

"She *is* lovely," said Percy Jones to Daphne amid the convivial din. They were watching Janice pose for the photographer. She was wearing the silvery full-length gown that Daphne had spent several hours altering. The blue ribbon and fat yellow medal hung crudely against the whiteness of her throat.

"She's a handful," said Daphne.

"Mmm," said Percy Jones.

"Down boy," said Daphne with an effusiveness brought out by champagne and the fact that she did not know Percy Jones. She was aware that, apart from being well over 50, he was an organist.

"I've hardly slept all week. Between getting her fed and watered and dressed and on time and warmed up. And massaged. She can't play without having half her body massaged. I still can't believe she's won. I've been a basket-case ever since the semi-finals. I get so (effing) nervous. *She's* been as cool as a cuke marching uphill in January but you know what? She hasn't really been playing as well as she can. Not really."

"I admire your devotion," said Percy Jones, turning toward Daphne. "I've been teaching for god knows how long. I've had good students of course, but never one with...the spark. Never one even with the promise of becoming a better organist than I am. If I were to get one now, I really wonder if I'd have the energy to...well to do what you've done with Janice. The patience, the encou...."

"Where is she?" said Daphne.

Janice was nowhere to be seen. Daphne hurried over to the photographer who was now taking pictures of the runners-up. He indicated the washroom.

There was a white-gloved woman wearing earrings as big as mints posted outside the washroom door.

"She asked me to bring her," said the woman. "She said she would be all right by herself inside."

"Thanks," said Daphne, going in.

Janice was supporting herself against a sink.

"Sorry. I lost track of you," said Daphne. "Mille pardons. Are you all done? I was listening to this somewhat slithery but otherwise quite hunkish old organist sing your praises and I just sort of...."

"Get out of my *sight*," hissed Janice.

And then she laughed tightly at her little piece of cleverness.

Hockey. They loved to listen to hockey on television, Janice constantly trying to soothe Daphne's aggressive deriding of even their favourite players. She had a remarkable memory, Janice did, for hockey players' names and statistics. She also had an excellent memory for hockey gossip—which players were still available, which players had gone to jail for being with underage girls, which players were sleeping with which players' wives and so on—but her information was spurious, invented by Daphne as she read, supposedly, from the sports pages.

Camden, New Hampshire. The White Mountain Motel. Janice, in her excitement to put on her newly acquired extra-large T-shirt, banged her elbow against a lamp bolted to the floor.

"OOOoooo," she moaned, finding a bed and lying down on it. "Pain o pain o pain."

"Daphne," she said after her elbow had cooled, "I've never been so exHAUsted in all my life. Never. Not EVer."

Her head was waggling and her gaping mouth made her nose wrinkle. Daphne had never seen her so extravagantly happy.

"Tell me, Moby, what name would you give to your darkness right now?" she said.

"You reMEMber," said Janice. "Mmmmmm.... Perseverance."

"And what's it like?"

"Oh I don't know. It's TIRED."

And again Daphne was disappointed. She regretted having asked about this naming darkness, and she resolved not to ask again.

Janice was fingering the vinyl letters printed onto her T-shirt.

"They feel like dried mud," she said. "THIS...BODY... CLIMBED...MOUNT WASHINGTON."

The Prelude in D minor, Fugue in A minor. The waiting darkness was breathing and hot in Redpath Hall. Janice had started in playing a little too fast. She was struggling against the guitar. The back of her neck was tense, her left thumb was aching, perspiration crawled down her armpit.

The darkness, sensing her vulnerability, began quickly to invade her, pushing its way silently into her mouth and ears and up her nose.

Until there was silence everywhere. Her hands and memory, the air, the audience, all were silent. She had stopped playing. She was lost.

"There's so much music to learn," said Janice in response to the interviewer's question. "A blind person you see has to remember it all, all the time, doesn't he. He has to rehearse everything continually in order not to forget. But there's so much music. So much. Really. So much. It's not possible. Do you think?"

"I'm sure I don't know," said the interviewer gently. "But teaching, you enjoy teaching do you?"

"Oh I love teaching," said Janice.

Java. Swarms of Indonesians with dreamy eyes and small, pointless smiles. Lean, accommodating, smooth-faced insects.

The two travelled every summer now, becoming more adventurous with each season. They had many students between them, although Daphne taught far more than half.

And now they were listening to their guide in the pink-floored and poorly lit hall that shuddered with the moaning of elderly men huddled at the far end, praying. The air was hot and moist and smelled of breathing animals. Black moss outlined the glimmering blue tiles that covered the walls. The guide was explaining to them the use of the *kukuri*.

"As you see," he was saying, "the *kukuri* is a sort of brush, the hairs are quite long and extracted from the tail of the buffalo and the handle too is very often made from the horn of the buffalo. The old men strike themselves in the face," he said, using rapid flicks of the wrist to make the tips of the hairs of the *kukuri* grate lightly across first one cheek, and then the other. "This they are doing for some time after which they are in a sort of trance, you see, they are still doing everything as they should be but they do not feel pain. And so they choose this moment to light the *soaka* which is a lamp but very very bright, a quite, quite bright lamp. They look very hard at the *soaka* you see, for some minutes and then they are blind."

"Fascinating," said Janice.

"And are all these men blind?" asked Daphne, moved by a need to hear her own voice.

"They have all used the *kukuri* yes," said the guide. "When they are old. It is a very great honour, you see. To use the eyes to observe only the inner person."

"And how long," said Janice, "must they flick themselves in the face with the buffalo-hair brush before entering into this trance-like state?"

"Oh not so many hours, yes," said the guide. "Not so many."

"Really," said Janice. The eagerness of her manner appalled Daphne who felt repulsed by the exotic masochism of the ritual, the animal odour in the monastery and the bobbing intonation of the guide's voice.

"Could you," asked Janice, "light the *soaka* for me? I cannot help thinking I might perhaps be able to see it."

"Oh I could yes," said the guide, "because you are so blind. But you, misses," indicating Daphne, "must put your hands on top of your eyes."

The *soaka* burst into light, extremely white and intense, and died almost immediately. Daphne, peeking between her fingers, had to turn her head away sharply.

"What's in it that burns so brightly?" she asked.

"It is this white powders, you see, which we in Indonesian are calling 'tears of the leopard.' This is a very old name and not very true. Quite fanciful I think. And you, misses, did you see the *soaka*?"

"I am not sure," said Janice, extremely agitated. "I think I may have. Would it be possible to taste a bit of the powder?"

"Oh Janice, really!" said Daphne.

"Yes," said the guide, "yes, yes." He licked his finger, poked it into the lamp, and when he brought it out, the white powder clung to its tip. "A little," he said. "On the tongue. So."

Daphne could not help but watch as the guide touched his finger to Janice's blind, protruding tongue.

"You may swallow so little," he said. "Because you are so blind. You will understand better the *soaka*."

"You see," went on the guide, "the blindness of the *soaka* is not your blindness. It is a blindness of much light, not little. You, I think, live in the darkness."

"You, I think, talk too much," said Daphne.

"No," said Janice, a smooth and dreamy-eyed expression on her eyeless face, "it's fascinating. Really. Go on. Please."

"But that is all now," said the guide, smiling. "And so we go out."

All her life, Janice had difficulty releasing gas, a difficulty that became more acute as she grew older. So that by the time she had reached her middle thirties, she was susceptible to paralyzing cramps. To relieve this condition, it became necessary for Daphne to massage her abdomen every evening.

It did not matter whether Daphne were very tired, or feeling ill, she could not escape these sessions which, in general, were conducted in a silence broken only by a certain amount of internal gurgling and the soft flutter of air being released into the atmosphere.

Sometimes, though, they timed Janice's farts by solmization. As soon as they heard the characteristic hiss, they began singing "do, re, mi, fa," etc., stopping when the hiss died out. Even a short fart lasted at least an octave and some were so long that Daphne could not sing high enough and was left breathlessly mouthing the last syllables.

Nevertheless, Daphne was alarmed at how dry Janice was becoming. Her body seemed to be shrinking inside the loose skin. The numerous dark moles looked to Daphne like the heads of tacks holding the skin to the bone. The skin itself came away in flakes under Daphne's hands so that she took to dribbling baby oil along the small of Janice's bumpy spine and onto her midriff, and this made Janice shiver and squeal with anger.

Dear Miss MacMillan,
My son Donald has been taking guitar lessons from your associate, Miss Janice Kaas, for over two years now. Today, when he arrived home from his lesson, I noticed that his ear was bleeding. When questioned about this, he told me that Miss Kaas attaches clothes-pegs to his ears and pulls on them every time he makes a mistake. I examined his ears and found them to be swollen and callused. I cannot tell you, Miss MacMillan, how offensive it is to me that such methods are employed in this day and age. In view of Miss Kaas' condition, I will not pursue this matter further, but I can assure you that my son will never again set foot....

A live radio program. Janice was talking with the host in the cork-lined studio while Daphne listened outside on a monitor. Janice had been invited to appear on the show inasmuch as she was blind, had very nearly become a concert guitarist and was now a highly regarded teacher. She was saying that she had no regrets although she had had to live alone, with Daphne MacMillan of course, but essentially alone, and that she had not been able to participate in the world of men and done all the things that that would have allowed her to do, although of course she could have if she'd really wanted to perhaps but it was so very much more difficult for the visually impaired wasn't it, but still she was proud of her accomplishments and so on. And then she was going on to say that she did regret one thing, she would have so much liked to have had children, a woman who had not had children could not consider herself truly fulfilled, and it was at this point that Daphne stormed into the studio and spat, "You ungrateful bitch!" before the host had time to put his hand over the microphone.

Janice had stopped eating. She did not even have the energy to use her blindness to defy Daphne. It was as if her darkness had turned into a pink-scented fog that neither interested nor displeased her.

Daphne would lie for hours in the upper berth of the heavy bunk beds they had bought years before when they had moved into their duplex—because the bedrooms were too small for two beds and because Janice could not fall asleep alone—and listen in vain for the familiar snortings and squeals, the kickings and brief cries of a life straining against sleep. They did not come. Janice slept peaceably on, exhaling with relentless precision as the large red numbers of the clock-radio silently changed.

So Daphne went to a grocery store and bought every bag of marshmallows, and on bath night, she emptied them all into the bathtub.

And when Janice came into the bathroom holding the Royal Doulton back-scrubbing brush she had purchased in a luxury boutique in Manchester, she asked:

"Have you run the bath?"

"Of course I have," said Daphne.

"It doesn't smell like it."

Daphne took her by the free hand and led her to the bathtub. "Foot up."

"Are you sure?" said Janice.

"Foot up," said Daphne.

Janice had lifted her leg over the edge of the tub when she became alarmed.

"No no no," she said. She tried to pull her leg out, but in so doing lost her balance and instead plunged her foot deep into the marshmallows. She screamed, wildly swinging the heavy china brush which rattled against the tiles, beat into the plastic curtain and clipped Daphne on the nose.

Howling, Daphne took hold of Janice by the waist and down they fell into the bathtub, Daphne yelling that it was just marshmallows, marshmallows, marshmallows, just a joke, a j, o, k, e, until Janice sat in an awkward slouch against the taps, shivering with bleak, little sobs.

Daphne, blood still dripping from the tip of her nose, her face and scalp throbbing, regarded Janice, saw the jumble of her bones in the sunless skin, saw the small, pointless breasts, the crinkled face glazed with tears. A dying bird to be scooped up by any child, and thrown away with excited disgust.

"What did you do that for?" whimpered Janice.

"I don't know," said Daphne. "You *love* marshmallows."

"You can't stand to be left out can you," muttered Janice.

"What?" said Daphne.

But Janice kept quiet. And then she picked up a marshmallow and started to nibble on it.

"It tastes like blood," she said.

"Yes well you kind of clobbered me with your brush. I've leaked several nosefuls all over your nice white marshmallows. They're all kind of pink."

Janice attempted unskillfully to spit out the marshmallow. It dribbled down her chin, which she wiped quickly with her hand.

So Daphne got up out of the bathtub then.

"Where are you going?" said Janice.

"Fishing," said Daphne.

"I want you to get me out now," said Janice.

"Go stew," said Daphne.

"I don't know what pink means," said Janice. "I don't want to stay here."

"Stew in my blood a while anyway," said Daphne, rejoicing.

"Well, what did I do," said Daphne in response to the interviewer's question. "I stared. I just stared. I did that for about seven months and then I took up smoking. Which was VERy stupid because now I can't stop. And after that, well I started playing the guitar again. I had been teaching all the time of course, when Moby was alive I mean, but I hadn't been playing very much. Moby was a terrible snob you know. She would never play duets with me. She couldn't even stand to hear me practice. If I wanted to get in an hour or two, I had to get up in the middle of the night, go down to the basement and close myself in the bathroom. It's true. But she had a right to be a snob. She was an absolutely brilliant guitarist as you well know...she didn't play a note, she etched it.... She would undoubtedly have had an international career had it not been for her memory problems. But I mean why should she get up in front of a bunch of people just waiting for her to suffer a memory lapse so they could say aahhhhh the poor thing, the poor poor thing, the poor poor thing thing."

"Yes. But *you* have an international career now."

"Let's not go diving off the shark-infested deep-end. On my last tour of England I gave mostly noon-hour concerts for little old ladies like myself. Except that I'm not so little anymore."

"But you've also done the U.S. And Germany. And your Villa-Lobos disc is highly acclaimed. Many people feel it's among the best recordings made in Canada this year."

"Many people are very nice."

"And how do you explain that a snow-bound Canadian sensibility can so well enter into the rich Brazilian rhythms of Villa-Lobos?"

"Well now that *is* a lot of balls. Really. Villa-Lowblows is a wonderful wonderful composer. Despite his smelly cigars. I just let him take my hand and try to keep up with him."

Daphne MacMillan, 62, Professor of Music, sat in her, as she called it, bite-sized condominium that smelled heavily of the same carpet that had lain in her music-room for many years.

She thought how curious it was that her resolve was so firm, considering that until short minutes ago, she had not once thought of doing what she was about to do. And yet it was so simple and obvious, like the explanation to any good trick.

But it was important to her to have a name. Not crucial. Impermanence would do perhaps. Impermanence. Imperm. Anence.

Janice, Janice, Janice. Beautiful and overblown to the bitter end.

It was odd. She had always thought she would become reflective in her old age. She had always thought old people were reflective. But most of the time there wasn't much of anything going on inside her head.

Years went by as quickly as months had used to. At this rate, she thought, she would be 70 by September.

So it did not matter if her life had been wasted. Because it had now been lived. Life *is* a sort of trick, she thought. Once it's over you're left wondering how it was done. A good trick. Not good good. Good effective.

Impermanence. A musical name at least.

Janice, Janice. Dead at 42. A dry white slouch with a bowel full of driving cancer cells. Diagnosed and dead all in a week.

My darkness is not always the same, she thought. She could easily smell the chocolate warming. Sometimes it is very smooth. Sometimes it rustles. Sometimes it seems on the verge of disappearing. A trick of the memory.

No. She did not like impermanence.

It was Janice's name, not Daphne's. And Daphne had, as it were, figured out how her trick was done.

There was a time, she thought, when she would have been appalled at the idea that life was nothing but a trick. Those were the days of course when she worried that she wasn't eating in enough French restaurants and seeing enough Japanese films, not drinking strong enough coffee, not touching enough, not being touched enough. And here Daphne smiled. Those were the days when she read women's magazines by the handful in order to prove to herself that she wasn't living her life properly. And again, Daphne smiled with an eagerness that was unquestionably a form of joy. For in another region of her thinking, she had found her name, although she had not as yet admitted it to herself. There, she was remembering exactly where she had placed the can of beans, and the can-opener, the pot, the bread, and, of course, the butter, the butter. Her first meal in her new last life.

Those were the days, she thought, when she would have been revolted at the sight of her 60-year-old self dropping cigarette ash onto her tweed suit, childless, loveless, clutching her little statuette for Best Classical Solo Recording by a Female Artist Living in a Pink Fog.

And so it was the appropriate moment to begin. She took up the *kukuri* that Janice had so insisted on buying—

although they had not been for sale and she had only been allowed one because she was blind and, of course, willing to pay an arm and both legs—the *kukuri* that she had taken down from the china cabinet along with the *soaka*, and, holding the horn handle loosely, flicked her wrist rapidly so that the tips of the hairs of the *kukuri* grated lightly across her cheek.

Janice, Janice, Janice. Naming her darkness for the last time. With her dead eyes and her fetid breath. I can see it growing inside me, Daphne. It beats like a heart. It is my darkness and its name is faithlessness. Its name is impermanence.

Janice, Janice, Janice, thought Daphne. Beautiful and overblown to the bitter end.

Janice, she said. I do not understand your names. They're weird polysyllabic names I think. Heartless. They're too much like you.

And here, Daphne flicked her wrist again so that the *kukuri* grated across her other cheek. She was terribly excited.

Listen Moby, she said. I have figured out how all my tricks are done so to speak. And you, poor thing, never saw how any of yours were done. And again, she flicked the *kukuri*. I have my name. Not that it matters because you won't like my name. And anyway my darkness will really be a lightness won't it. Again flicking the *kukuri*. But I might as well tell you its name will be very good butter. Do you like it? Again, flicking. Very good butter. No, well I told you you wouldn't. And again, flicking. But wait for me, Moby. I'll be along before too many moons have passed and we can play some of those Emilio Poo-hole duets. And again. The duets you wished you could find a partner for and afterwards you can give *me* the back-rub for once. And again. And we can dream up names together till the cows come over the hill, over and over the hill, again and again. And again.

MARCUS YOUSSEF's first play, *A Line in the Sand* (co-written with Guillermo Verdecchia), won the 1997 Floyd S. Chalmers Canadian Play Award. His most recent play, *Mr. Bill*, was broadcast by CBC Radio in 1998. He is currently living on Saltspring Island.

MARY SWAN attended York University and the University of Guelph, and spent several years travelling in Europe and the Middle East. Her stories have appeared in *The Malahat Review*, *The Ontario Review*, *Best Canadian Stories* and *Sudden Fiction*. She lives in Guelph with her husband and daughter.

JOHN LAVERY lives in Gatineau, Quebec, with his wife and three children. He has been a cartographer, a survey technician, a draftsman and a ship's officer, and now divides his time between fathering and writing. A first collection of stories is forthcoming.

MAGGIE HELWIG was born in Liverpool, England and grew up in Kingston, Ontario. She edits an occasional litzine and has published one book of essays, a collection of stories and five books of poetry. She has also worked with a variety of peace and human-rights organizations in Canada and England. She now lives in Toronto with her partner Ken Simons and their daughter Simone Helwig.

Previous volumes in this series contained stories by the following writers:

1998: Leona Theis, Gabriella Goliger and Darryl Whetter
1997: Elyse Gasco, Dennis Bock and Nadine McInnis
1996: Lewis DeSoto, Murray Logan and Kelley Aitken
1995: Warren Cariou, Marilyn Gear Pilling and François Bonneville
1994: Donald McNeill, Elise Levine and Lisa Moore
1993: Gayla Reid, Hannah Grant and Barbara Parkin
1992: Caroline Adderson, Marilyn Eisenstat and Marina Endicott
1991: Ellen McKeough, Robert Majzels and Patricia Seaman
1990: Peter Stockland, Sara McDonald and Steven Heighton
1989: Brian Burke, Michelle Heinemann and Jean Rysstad
1988: Christopher Fisher, Carol Anne Wien and Rick Hillis
1987: Charles Foran, Patricia Bradbury and Cynthia Holz
1986: Dayv James-French, Lesley Krueger and Rohinton Mistry
1985: Sheila Delany, Frances Itani and Judith Pond
1984: Diane Schoemperlen, Joan Fern Shaw and Michael Rawdon
1983: Sharon Butala, Bonnie Burnard and Sharon Sparling
1982: Barry Dempster, Don Dickinson and Dave Margoshes
1981: Peter Behrens, Linda Svendsen and Ernest Hekkanen
1980: Martin Avery, Isabel Huggan and Mike Mason

Most of these books are still available. Please inquire.